The Elements of Style

從句子到文章

英語章法

威廉・史壯克 William Strunk Jr. 原著
楊簞璐 譯著

從細節到整體，幫助你寫出精準、
簡潔且兼具說服力的文章

精準的文法與嚴謹的結構，是專業英文寫作的基石
從規則到風格，全面提升你的文字表達力與專業度

目 錄

前言	005
Part 1　運用與組合規則	007
Part 2　格式與用詞規範	107
Part 3　寫作風格入門	211
參考書目	273

前言

　　《英語章法：從句子到文章》是筆者對 *The Elements of Style* 英文原作的逐段翻譯。全書對原作結構做了調整，分為三個板塊，分別介紹：英語詞句的運用與組合規則，格式與用詞規範以及對個人寫作風格形成的初步探討。*The Elements of Style* 這本書流傳了一個世紀，被尊為「英文寫作聖經」，書中貫穿了一種「作者應該為讀者負責」的思想，也就是英語寫作力求「簡」、「明」，以讓文章更容易被人讀懂。要做到這一點，我們需要不斷錘鍊自己的語言，在追求個性化表達的同時也不忘規範化，是「戴著腳鐐跳舞」。

楊箪璐

前言

Part 1　運用與組合規則

1-1 單數名詞的所有格

> Rule 1
> Form the possessive singular of nouns by adding 's
> 規則一　要透過新增 's 來構成單數名詞的所有格

Follow this rule whatever the final consonant.

無論該單數名詞的結尾子音字母是什麼，都遵從此規則。

例如：

Charles's friend 【查理的朋友】

Burns's poems 【彭斯的詩】

the witch's malice 【女巫的惡意】

補充說明 1：例外的古代專有名詞

Exceptions are the possessives of ancient proper names ending in -es and -is.

例外情況是一些以 -es 和 -is 結尾的古代專有名詞的所有格，只加 '。

例如：

Jesus' 【耶穌的】

for conscience' sake 【為了良心】

for righteousness' sake 【為了正義】

But such forms as Moses' Laws, Isis' temple are commonly replaced by

但是諸如摩西律法、伊西斯神廟這些形式一般會被以下的形式取代

the laws of Moses 【摩西律法】

the temple of Isis 【伊西斯神廟】

補充說明 2：物主代詞和不定代詞

The pronominal possessives hers, its, theirs, yours, and ours have no apostrophe. Indefinite pronouns, however, use the apostrophe to show possession.

物主代詞 hers、its、theirs、yours 和 ours 不用縮略號表示所有格，但不定代詞要用。

例如：

one's rights 【某人的權利】

somebody else's umbrella 【別人的傘】

補充說明 3：常見錯誤 it's 和 its

A common error is to write it's for its, or vice versa. The first is a contraction, meaning "it is". The second is a possessive.

常見錯誤是把 it's 寫成 its，或反之。前一個是縮略形式，意思是「它是」。後一個是所有格。

例如：

It's a wise dog that scratches its own fleas. 【聰明的狗會自己抓跳蚤。】

1-2 並列多項的分隔

Rule 2　In a series of three or more terms with a single conjunction, use a comma after each term except the last

規則二　由一個連詞連線的一組三個或三個以上的語言片段，除最後一個外，每個語言片段之後都要有一個逗號（連詞放在最後一個片段之前）

This comma is often referred to as the "serial comma".

這種逗號通常被稱為「連續逗號」。

例如：

red, white, and blue 【紅的、白的和藍的】

gold, silver, or copper 【金、銀或銅】

He opened the letter, read it, and made a note of its contents. 【他拆開信，讀了，並記下了其中內容。】

補充說明：

In the names of business firms, the last comma is usually omitted. Follow the usage of the individual firm.

在公司名稱中，最後一個逗號通常刪除。依據各家公司慣例而定。

例如：

Little, Brown and Company Donaldson

Lufkin & Jenrette

1-3　插入語的分隔

Rule 3　Enclose parenthetic expressions between commas

規則三　要把插入語夾在兩個逗號間

例如：

The best way to see a country, unless you are pressed for time, is to travel on foot.【欣賞一個國家最好的方式，如果你不趕時間的話，是步行。】

補充說明 1：很難判斷一個片段是不是插入語。

This rule is difficult to apply; it is frequently hard to decide whether a single word, such as however, or a brief phrase is or is not parenthetic.

這條規則較難使用；因為通常很難確定一個單字（如however）或一個片語是否是插入語。

補充說明 2：插入語也可以不用逗號。

If the interruption to the flow of the sentence is but slight, the commas may be safely omitted.

如果句子的插入語較短，不用逗號也沒關係。

1-3　插入語的分隔

補充說明 3：插入語前後不能只用一個逗號。

But whether the interruption is slight or considerable, never omit one comma and leave the other. There is no defense for such punctuation as:

但是無論句子的插入語長還是短,都不能在原本兩個逗號中刪除一個,而只留下一個。以下句子中的逗號使用是說不通的:

例如：

Marjorie's husband, Colonel Nelson paid us a visit yesterday. (✗)【瑪喬麗的丈夫,尼爾森上校昨天來拜訪了我們。】

My brother you will be pleased to hear, is now in perfect health. (✗)【我弟弟你一定會很高興聽到,現在十分健康。】

補充說明 4：關於時間書寫中的逗號使用。

Dates usually contain parenthetic words or figures. Punctuate as follows:

日期的書寫中通常包括插入的詞或數字。標點符號如下:

例如：

February to July, 1992　【1992 年 2 月到 7 月】

April 6, 1986　【1986 年 4 月 6 日】

Wednesday, November 14, 1990　【1990 年 11 月 14 日,星期三】

注意：

Note that it is customary to omit the comma.

若按慣例順序書寫，即日月年，則可省略逗號。

例如：

6 April 1988 【1988 年 4 月 6 日】

The last form is an excellent way to write a date; the figures are separated by a word and are, for that reason, quickly grasped.

最後這種書寫方式極好；兩個數字被一個單字隔開，一目了然。

補充說明 5：稱呼或頭銜書寫中的逗號使用。

A name or a title in direct address is parenthetic.

直接用於稱呼的名字或頭銜是插入語。

例如：

If, Sir, you refuse, I cannot predict what will happen. 【如果，先生，您拒絕，我就不能預料會發生什麼了。】

Well, Susan, this is a fine mess you are in. 【哎呀，蘇珊，妳的處境真是糟透了。】

補充說明 6：縮寫形式書寫中逗號的使用。

The abbreviations etc., i. e., and e. g., the abbreviations for academic degrees, and titles that follow a name are parenthetic

1-3 插入語的分隔

and should be punctuated accordingly.

縮寫形式的 etc.（等等）、i. e.（即）和 e. g.（例如），在姓名後面的縮寫形式學位、頭銜也是插入語，也有相應的標點要求。

例如：

Letters, packages, etc., should go here. 【信件、包裹等應該放在這裡。】

Horace Fulsome, Ph.D., presided. 【哲學博士霍瑞思‧福爾索姆主持。】

Rachel Simonds, Attorney 【瑞秋‧蒙茲律師】

The Reverend Harry Lang, S. J. 【耶穌會哈利‧朗牧師】

No comma, however, should separate a noun from a restrictive term of identification.

一個中心名詞和表示其身分的限制性片段之間，不能用逗號隔開。

例如：

Billy the Kid 【比利小子】

The novelist Jane Austen 【小說家珍‧奧斯汀】

William the Conqueror 【征服者威廉】

The poet Sappho 【詩人莎芙】

Although Junior, with its abbreviation Jr., has commonly been regarded as parenthetic, logic suggests that it is, in fact, restrictive and therefore not in need of a comma.

儘管表示「小……」的 Junior 一詞及其縮略式 Jr. 通常被認為是插入語，但事實上，卻是限制性片段，無需逗號。

例如：

James Wright Jr. 【小詹姆士·懷特】

補充說明 7：非限定性定語從句書寫中逗號的使用。

Nonrestrictive relative clauses are parenthetic, as are similar clauses introduced by conjunctions indicating the time or the place. Commas are therefore needed. A nonrestrictive clause is one that does not serve to identify or define the antecedent noun.

非限定性關係從句是插入語，和由表時間、地點的連詞引導的從句一樣。因此要用逗號隔開。非限定性從句不是先行詞的同位語或定義。

例如：

The audience, which had at first been indifferent, became more and more interested. 【觀眾們，最初反應冷淡，後來變得越來越感興趣。】

In 1769, when Napoleon was born, Corsica had but recently

been acquired by France.【1769 年，拿破崙誕生時，科西嘉島剛被法國占領。】

Nether Stowey, where Coleridge wrote *The Rime of the Ancient Mariner*, is a few miles from Bridgewater.【下斯托伊，柯勒律治創作《古舟子詠》的地方，離布里奇沃特僅有幾英里遠。】

In these sentences, the clauses introduced by which, when, and where are nonrestrictive; they do not limit or define; they merely add something. In the first example, the clause introduced by which does not serve to tell which of several possible audiences is meant; the reader presumably knows that already. The clause adds, parenthetically, a statement supplementing that in the main clause. Each of the three sentences is a combination of two statements that might have been made independently.

在這些句子中，由 which、when、where 引導的從句都是非限定性的；它們不起限制或定義的作用，只是補充說明一些內容。在第一個例句中，假定讀者已經知道觀眾 audience 具體指哪些人，而由 which 引導的從句，並不是用來界定哪些人是觀眾的。這個從句只是以插入語的方式，對主句的一些相關資訊進行補充說明。上述的三個例句，都是相對獨立的兩個敘述片段的組合，是可以拆分開的。

Part 1　運用與組合規則

例如：

The audience was at first indifferent.【觀眾最初是冷漠的。】

Later it became more and more interested.【後來變得越來越感興趣。】

Napoleon was born in 1769.【拿破崙生於 1769 年。】

At that time Corsica had but recently been acquired by France.【在那時科西嘉島剛被法國占領。】

Coleridge wrote *The Rime of the Ancient Mariner* at Nether Stowey.【柯勒律治在下斯托伊創作了《古舟子詠》。】

Nether Stowey is a few miles from Bridgewater.【下斯托伊離布里奇沃特僅有幾英里遠。】

補充說明 8：限定性關係從句書寫中不用逗號。

Restrictive clauses, by contrast, are not parenthetic and are not set off by commas.

相對地，限定性關係從句不是插入語，不能用逗號與先行詞隔開。

例如：

People who live in glass houses shouldn't throw stones.【住玻璃房子的人不應該扔石頭。（比喻自己有某種短處的人不要去攻擊別人的類似短處。）】

Here the clause introduced by who does serve to tell which people are meant; the sentence, unlike the sentences above, cannot be split into two independent statements.

這個由 who 引導的從句是用來界定 people 含義的，與之前的句子不同，不能夠分割成兩個獨立的敘述。也就是說，先行詞 people 是一個空泛的類別詞，沒有後面的定語從句界定，意思就不完整了。

補充說明 9：分詞片語和同位語書寫中逗號的使用。

The same principle of comma use applies to participial phrases and to appositives.

在分詞片語和同位語中，逗號的適用原則也一樣，要看是限定還是非限定。

例如：

People sitting in the rear couldn't hear. (restrictive) 【坐在後面的人聽不見。（限定性）】

Uncle Bert, being slightly deaf, moved forward. (nonrestrictive) 【伯特叔叔，有點耳聾，挪到前面了。（非限定性）】

My cousin Bob is a talented harpist. (restrictive) 【我的表兄鮑勃是一位有才華的豎琴師。（限定性）】

Our oldest daughter, Mary, sings. (nonrestrictive) 【我們的大女兒，瑪麗，唱歌。（非限定性）】

補充說明 10：插入語位於句首時，書寫中逗號的使用。

When the main clause of a sentence is preceded by a phrase or a subordinate clause, use a comma to set off these elements.

當主句之前有片語或從句時，要用逗號分隔開。

例如：

Partly by hard fighting, partly by diplomatic skill, they enlarged their dominions to the east and rose to royal rank with the possession of Sicily. 【部分透過艱苦戰鬥，部分透過外交手段，他們向東擴展了帝國版圖並因占領西西里加官晉爵。】

1-4　獨立從句分隔（1）

Rule 4　Place a comma before a conjunction introducing an independent clause

規則四　要在引導獨立從句的連詞前使用逗號

例如：

The early records of the city have disappeared, and the story of its first years can no longer be reconstructed. 【這座城市的早

期文獻記載已經遺失,而它早年的歷史也無法重建。】

The situation is perilous, but there is still one chance of escape.【情況非常危險,但仍有機會逃脫。】

補充說明 1:用逗號與主句隔開的副詞從句。

Two-part sentences of which the second member is introduced by as (in the sense of "because"), for, or, nor, or while (in the sense of "and at the same time") likewise require a comma before the conjunction.

由兩個分句組成的句子,如果其中第二個分句是由連詞 as(因為)、for、or、nor 或者 while(當……時)引導的,這些連詞前同樣要用逗號。

補充說明 2:從句套從句的情況。

If a dependent clause, or an introductory phrase requiring to be set off by a comma, precedes the second independent clause, no comma is needed after the conjunction.

如果一個非獨立從句,或者一個需要由逗號隔開的介紹性片語,位於第二個獨立分句之前,則連詞後不用逗號。

例如:

The situation is perilous, but if we are prepared to act promptly, there is still one chance of escape.【情況非常危險,但如果我們準備好及時行動,仍有機會逃脫。】

補充說明 3：兩個從句主語相同的情況。

When the subject is the same for both clauses and is expressed only once, a comma is useful if the connective is but. When the connective is and, the comma should be omitted if the relation between the two statements is close or immediate.

兩個從句主語相同，省略第二個從句的主語時，若連詞是「but」，仍需用逗號隔開；但如果連詞是「and」，且兩個從句關係密切時，則不用。

例如：

I have heard the arguments, but am still unconvinced.【我聽了這些理論，但還是沒被說服。】

He has had several years' experience and is thoroughly competent.【他有多年經驗，完全可以勝任。】

1-5　獨立從句分隔（2）

Rule 5　Do not join independent clauses with a comma

規則五　不要用逗號連線兩個獨立從句

補充說明 1：三種解決方案。

(1) 無連詞，用分號。

If two or more clauses grammatically complete and not joined by a conjunction are to form a single compound sentence, the proper mark of punctuation is a semicolon.

兩個或兩個以上文法結構完整的從句組成合句，如果沒有連詞連線，中間的標點要用分號。

例如：

Mary Shelley's works are entertaining; they are full of engaging ideas. 【瑪麗·雪萊的作品是有趣的；其中充滿引人入勝的想法。】

It is nearly half past five; we cannot reach town before dark. 【快五點半了；我們天黑前進不了城了。】

(2) 拆兩句，用句號。

It is, of course, equally correct to write each of these as two sentences, replacing the semicolons with periods.

分號連線的兩個分句,直接寫成句號結尾的兩個句子也對。

例如:

Mary Shelley's works are entertaining.【瑪麗‧雪萊的作品是有趣的。】

They are full of engaging ideas.【作品充滿引人入勝的想法。】

It is nearly half past five.【快五點半了。】

We cannot reach town before dark.【我們天黑前進不了城了。】

(3) 有連詞,用逗號。

If a conjunction is inserted, the proper mark is a comma. (Rule 4)

從句前如有連詞,就用逗號。

例如:

Mary Shelley's works are entertaining, for they are full of engaging ideas.【瑪麗‧雪萊的作品是有趣的,因為其中充滿引人入勝的想法。】

It is nearly half past five, and we cannot reach town before dark. 【快五點半了,而我們天黑前進不了城了。】

A comparison of the three forms given above will show clearly the advantage of the first. It is, at least in the examples given, better than the second form because it suggests the close relationship between the two statements in a way that the second does not attempt, and better than the third because it is briefer and therefore more forcible. Indeed, this simple method of indicating relationship between statements is one of the most useful devices of composition. The relationship, as above, is commonly one of cause and consequence.

比較上述三種解決方案,第一種具有明顯優勢。至少在給出的這些例句範圍內如此。因為第一種較之於第二種,更能展現兩個句子的密切關係,較之於第三種,更簡潔有力。的確,這種用分號來表明兩個句子間關係的簡單做法,是最有用的寫作手法之一。而上述情況中,分號通常表明兩句之間有因果關係。

補充說明 2:

Note that if the second clause is preceded by an adverb, such as accordingly, besides, then, therefore, or thus, and not by a conjunction, the semicolon is still required.

Part 1　運用與組合規則

注意：如果第二個分句前沒有連詞，但是有副詞，諸如 accordingly、besides、then、therefore 或 thus 等，仍然要用分號（副詞和主句間往往用逗號分隔開）。也就是說，只要沒有連詞，就是不能用逗號。

例如：

I had never been in the place before; besides, it was dark as a tomb. 【我之前從沒到過這地方；此外，那裡黑得像墳墓。】

An exception to the semicolon rule is worth noting here. A comma is preferable when the clauses are very short and alike in form, or when the tone of the sentence is easy and conversational.

分號有個例外情況值得一提。如果兩個獨立從句短而且形式上對稱，或語氣隨意如同口語，則用逗號更好。

例如：

Man proposes, God disposes. 【謀事在人，成事在天。】

The gates swung apart, the bridge fell, and the portcullis was drawn up. 【城門開啟了，吊橋放下來了，閘門拉起來了。】

I hardly knew him, he was so changed. 【我幾乎沒認出他來，他變了那麼多。】

Here today, gone tomorrow. 【今天還在，明天淘汰。】

1-6　句子完結才用句號

Rule 6　Do not break sentences in two

規則六　不要把句子拆成兩半

In other words, do not use periods for commas.

換言之，該用逗號的地方不要用句號。

例如：

I met them on a Cunard liner many years ago. Coming home from Liverpool to New York.（✗）【很多年前，我在丘納德號輪船上遇到他們。在從利物浦回紐約的途中。】

She was an interesting talker. A woman who had traveled all over the world and lived in half a dozen countries.（✗）【她是一位說話很有趣的人。一位環遊世界並在六個國家居住過的女士。】

In both these examples, the first period should be replaced by a comma and the following word begins with a small letter.

在這兩組例句中，中間的句號都應改為逗號，其後單字首字母小寫。

Part 1　運用與組合規則

補充說明：文法結構不完整，但表示強調的片段單獨成句。

It is permissible to make an emphatic word or expression serve the purpose of a sentence and to punctuate it accordingly.

允許表強調的詞或片語單獨成句，並適用句號。

例如：

Again and again he called out. No reply. 【他一次次大聲呼喊。沒人回覆。】

The writer must, however, be certain that the emphasis is warranted, lest a clipped sentence seem merely a blunder in syntax or in punctuation. Generally speaking, the place for broken sentences is in dialogue, when a character happens to speak in a clipped or fragmentary way.

但是，作者必須要確保這種強調有特定語境，以免這種單獨成句的語言片段看起來只是句法或標點錯誤。一般來講，片段成句常用於：在對話中，談話一方偶爾說出的隻言片語。

Rules 3, 4, 5, and 6 cover the most important principles that govern punctuation. They should be so thoroughly mastered that their application becomes second nature.

規則三、四、五、六覆蓋了標點斷句的最重要原則，應該徹底掌握，運用自如。

1-7　冒號的提示作用

> Rule 7　Use a colon after an independent clause to introduce a list of particulars, an appositive, an amplification, or an illustrative quotation
>
> 規則七　要在獨立分句之後用冒號,來引出一系列具體項目、一個同位語、一項引申或一個解釋性引語

A colon tells the reader that what follows is closely related to the preceding clause.

冒號說明其前後語片密切相關。

補充說明 1:冒號的斷句功能與分號、破折號比較。

The colon has more effect than the comma, less power to separate than the semicolon, and more formality than the dash.

冒號斷句效果比逗號強,但比分號弱,比破折號更正式。

補充說明 2:冒號不能分隔的成分。

It usually follows an independent clause and should not separate a verb from its complement or a preposition from its object. The examples in the left-hand column, below, are wrong; they should be rewritten as in the right-hand column.

冒號通常用於獨立分句後。冒號不能用於分隔動詞和補語，也不能分隔介詞和介詞賓語。下列左邊一欄的例句是錯的，應該被改寫為右邊一欄的樣子。

例如：

Your dedicated whittler requires: a knife, a piece of wood, and a back porch. (✗)【你那位專心致志的削木工需要三樣東西：一把小刀、一根木料和一個後廊。】	Your dedicated whittler requires three props: a knife, a piece of wood, and a back porch. (✓)【你那位專心致志的削木工需要三樣東西：一把小刀、一根木料和一個後廊。】
Understanding is that penetrating quality of knowledge that grows from: theory, practice, conviction, assertion, error, and humiliation. (✗)【理解是參透知識的本質，這些知識來自理論、實踐、信念、確證、錯誤和羞辱。】	Understanding is that penetrating quality of knowledge that grows from theory, practice, conviction, assertion, error, and humiliation. (✓)【理解是參透知識的本質，這些知識來自理論、實踐、信念、確證、錯誤和羞辱。】

1-7 冒號的提示作用

補充說明 3：冒號也可以出現在特定的兩個獨立從句之間。

Join two independent clauses with a colon if the second interprets or amplifies the first.

如果後一個獨立從句是對前一個的解釋和擴展，中間可用冒號。

例如：

But even so, there was a directness and dispatch about animal burial: there was no stopover in the undertaker's foul parlor, no wreath or spray. 【但即便如此，動物葬禮還是直截了當的：無需在殯儀館停留，沒有花圈，也不用撒什麼。】

補充說明 4：冒號可以配合雙引號使用。

A colon may introduce a quotation that supports or contributes to the preceding clause.

冒號可以用來引出一個佐證冒號之前內容的直接引語。

例如：

The squalor of the streets reminded her of a line from Oscar Wilde: "We are all in the gutter, but some of us are looking at the stars." 【街道的骯髒讓她想起奧斯卡·王爾德的一句話：「儘管我們都身處陰溝中，但一些人仍在仰望星空。」】

補充說明 5：冒號的其他斷句功能。

The colon also has certain functions of form:

冒號還有一些特定的形式功能：

(1) to follow the salutation of a formal letter,

在正式信函的稱呼之後,

例如：

Dear Mr. Montague:【親愛的蒙塔古先生：】

(2) to separate hour from minute in a notation of time,

時間書寫中的小時和分鐘之間,

例如：

depart at 10:48 P. M.【下午 10：48 出發】

(3) and to separate the title of a work from its subtitle or a *Bible* chapter from a verse.

書名和副標題之間,或《聖經》與其各章節名稱之間。

例如：

Practical Calligraphy: An Introduction to Italic Script【實用書法：斜體字入門】

Nehemiah 11:7【《聖經》尼希米記第十一章第七節】

1-8　破折號的作用

Rule 8　Use a dash to set off an abrupt break or interruption and to announce a long appositive or summary

規則八　要使用破折號表示突然中斷，以帶出一個較長的同位語，或做總結

補充說明 1：破折號與逗號、分號、圓括號的比較。

A dash is a mark of separation stronger than a comma, less formal than a colon, and more relaxed than parentheses.

破折號分隔作用比逗號強，但是不如分號正式，不如圓括號嚴謹。

例如：

His first thought on getting out of bed— if he had any thought at all— was to get back in again.【他下床後第一個念頭 ── 如果他還能有什麼念頭的話 ── 就是再回到床上去。】

The rear axle began to make a noise — a grinding, chattering, teeth-gritting rasp.【車的後輪軸開始發出響聲 ── 一種嘎吱嘎吱、卡塔卡塔和磨牙般的刺耳聲音。】

033

Part 1　運用與組合規則

The increasing reluctance of the sun to rise, the extra nip in the breeze, the patter of shed leaves dropping— all the evidences of fall drifting into winter were clearer each day.

【日出越來越遲，寒風格外刺骨，樹葉紛紛掉落——秋去冬來的跡象日益明顯。】

補充說明 2：破折號是不太常用的標點。

Use a dash only when a more common mark of punctuation seems inadequate.

只有在一般標點都不太恰當時，才有必要用破折號。

例如：

Her father's suspicions proved well-founded — it was not Edward she cared for— it was San Francisco.（✗）【她父親的懷疑被證明是有根據的。她喜歡的不是愛德華，而是舊金山。】

Her father's suspicions proved well-founded. It was not Edward she cared for, it was San Francisco.（✓）【她父親的懷疑被證明是有根據的。她喜歡的不是愛德華，而是舊金山。】

Violence — the kind you see on television — is not honestly violent — there lies its harm. (✗)【暴力，你在電視上看到的那種，其實不算暴力。但也有危害。】

Violence, the kind you see on television, is not honestly violent. There lies its harm.（√）【暴力，你在電視上看到的那種，其實不算暴力。但也有危害。】

1-9　主謂一致

Rule 9　The number of the subject determines the number of the verb

規則九　主語的單複數決定謂語動詞的單複數

補充說明 1：修飾成分不影響單複數。

Words that intervene between subject and verb do not affect the number of the verb.

介於主語和謂語動詞之間的詞（組）不影響謂語動詞的單複數。

Part 1　運用與組合規則

例如：左邊句子主語是單數，但是受複數形式的修飾語影響，謂語動詞用了複數，是錯的，要改成右邊的樣子，即：

The bittersweet flavor of youth — its trials, its joys, its adventures, its challenges — are not soon forgotten.（✗）
【青春苦樂參半的味道——它的考驗、歡樂、冒險、挑戰——不會很快被遺忘。】

The bittersweet flavor of youth — its trials, its joys, its adventures, its challenges — is not soon forgotten.（√）
【青春苦樂參半的味道——它的考驗、歡樂、冒險、挑戰——不會很快被遺忘。】

補充說明 2：關係從句謂語。

A common blunder is the use of a singular verb form in a relative clause following "one of..." or a similar expression when the relative is the subject.

一個常見的錯誤是，關係從句的先行詞之前有「one of」一類的數量片語，而該從句的主語是關係代詞時，從句謂語動詞用了單數形式。

例如：比較下面兩組例句，左邊句子就是從句謂語用了單數形式的典型錯誤，要改成右邊的樣子，即：

one of the ablest scientists who has tacked this problem（✗）【解決這個問題的最有能力的科學家之一】

one of the ablest scientists who have tacked this problem（√）【解決這個問題的最有能力的科學家之一】

one of those people who is never ready on time（✗）【那些從不準時準備好的人之一】

one of those people who are never ready on time（√）【那些從不準時準備好的人之一】

補充說明 3：含有不定代詞的主語。

Use a singular verb form after each, either, everyone, everybody, neither, nobody, someone.

主語是 each、either、everyone、everybody、neither、nobody、someone 時，謂語動詞用單數。

例如：

Everybody thinks he has a unique sense of humor.【每個人都認為他有一種獨特的幽默感。】

Although both clocks strike cheerfully, neither keeps good time.【兩個鐘都敲得很歡樂，卻不準。】

補充說明 4：含有 none 的主語，分兩種情況討論。

With none, use the singular verb when the word means "no one" or "not one". A plural verb is commonly used when none suggests more than one thing or person.

對於 none 這個詞，如果其意思指「沒有一個」或「一個也不」時，謂語動詞用單數。而當 none 表示一個以上的人或事物時，謂語動詞通常用複數。

例如：

None of us is perfect.【我們中沒有人是完美的。】

None of us are perfect.【我們都不是完美的。】

None are so fallible as those who are sure they're right.【沒有人比那些確信自己是對的人更容易犯錯了。】

補充說明 5：複合主語，也分兩種情況討論。

(1) A compound subject formed of two or more nouns joined by and almost always requires a plural verb. But certain compounds, often clichés, are so inseparable they are considered a unit and so take a singular verb, as do compound subjects qualified by each or every.

兩個或兩個以上名詞以 and 連線組成複合主語時，幾乎總是要求謂語動詞用複數。但是一些特定的複合主語，通常是一些約定俗成的說法，被看作是固定搭配的一個整體，就像被 each 或 every 修飾的複合主語一樣，謂語動詞要用單數。

例如：

The walrus and the carpenter were walking close at hand. 【海象和木匠緊鄰著走過。】

The long and the short of it is... 【它的特點／要點是……】

Bread and butter was all she served. 【她端上來的就只有牛油配麵包。】

Give and take is essential to a happy household. 【相互遷就對於幸福的家庭至關重要。】

Every window, picture, and mirror was smashed. 【每一扇窗戶、每一幅畫、每一面鏡子都被砸碎了。】

補充說明 6：介詞片語修飾的單數主語。

A singular subject remains singular even if other nouns are connected to it by with, as well as, in addition to, except, together with, and no less than.

一個單數主語，其後即使有介詞 with、as well as、in addition to、except、together with 以及 no less than 引入其他名詞與之相連時，謂語動詞仍然用單數。

例如：

His speech as well as his manner is objectionable. 【他的言談舉止令人反感。】

Part 1　運用與組合規則

補充說明 7：連繫動詞。

A linking verb agrees with the number of its subject.

連繫動詞與其主語在單複數上要一致。

例如：

What is wanted is a few more pairs of hands.【所需要的是更多人手。】

The trouble with truth is its many varieties.【真理的麻煩在於它多變。】

補充說明 8：表面是複數實質含義為單數的主語。

Some nouns that appear to be plural are usually construed as singular and given a singular verb.

一些名詞表面上是複數，但通常被看作單數，謂語動詞也用單數。

例如：

Politics is an art, not a science.【政治是一門藝術，而非科學。】

The Republican Headquarters is on this side of the tracks.【共和黨總部就在路的這一邊。】

注意：headquarters 總部算單數，而 quarters 普通部門卻要算複數：

The general's quarters are across the river.【將軍的宿舍在河對面。】

In these cases the writer must simply learn the idioms. The contents of a book is singular. The contents of a jar may be either singular or plural, depending on what's in the jar — jam or marbles.

在這些案例中，作者必須要熟悉習慣用語。一本書的內容（contents），是單數；一個罐子裡的內容（contents），可以是單數，也可以是複數，取決於罐子裡裝了什麼 —— 果醬還是玻璃彈珠。

1-10　代詞的格

Rule 10　Use the proper case of pronoun
規則十　要正確使用代詞的「格」

The personal pronouns, as well as the pronoun who, change form as they function as subject or object.

人稱代詞以及 who，作主語時用主格；作賓語時用賓格。

例如：

The culprit, it turned out, was him. 【原來，罪魁禍首是他。】

We heavy eaters would rather walk than ride. 【我們食量大的人寧願走路也不搭車。】

Who knocks? 【誰敲門？】

Give this work to whoever looks idle. 【這工作誰閒給誰。】

In the last example, whoever is the subject of looks idle; the object of the preposition to is the entire clause whoever looks idle.

在最後一個例句中，looks idle 的主語是 whoever；介詞 to 的賓語是 whoever 引導的整個從句。

補充說明 1：who 與 whom 的選擇。

When who introduces a subordinate clause, its case depends on its function in that clause.

當 who 引導一個從句時，它的格取決於它在這個從句中作主語還是賓語。

例如：以下例句，左邊是錯誤的，應改為右邊的樣子。

Virgil Soames is the candidate whom we think will win.（✗）【維吉爾‧索姆斯是我們認為會獲勝的候選人。】

Virgil Soames is the candidate who we think will win. (We think he will win.)（√）【維吉爾‧索姆斯是我們認為會獲勝的候選人。（我們認為他會贏。）】

Virgil Soames is the candidate who we hope to elect.（✗）【維吉爾‧索姆斯是我們希望選出的候選人。】

Virgil Soames is the candidate whom we hope to elect. (We hope to elect him.)（√）【維吉爾‧索姆斯是我們希望選出的候選人。】

※ 在第一組例句中，who 是 will win 的主語，所以要用主格形式；而在第二組例句中，whom 是 elect 的賓語，所以要用賓格形式。

補充說明 2：比較從句中 than ＋介詞主格結構。

A pronoun in a comparison is nominative if it is the subject of a stated or understood verb.

比較從句的謂語往往與主句相同，不用說出來也能夠被理解，常被省略，所以 than 之後出現單獨一個代詞，實際上是連詞加一個句子主語，而不是介賓結構，注意要使用主格。

例如：

Sandy writes better than I. (Than I write.)【珊蒂寫得比我好。（比我寫得好。）】

※than 之後的謂語動詞一般不省略：

I think Horace admires Jessica more than I.（✗）【與我相比，我認為霍勒斯更欽佩潔西卡。】

I think Horace admires Jessica more than I do.（√）【我認為霍勒斯比我更欽佩潔西卡。】

Polly loves cake more than me.（✗）【比起我來，波莉更喜歡蛋糕。】

Polly loves cake more than she loves me.（√）【波莉愛蛋糕勝過愛我。】

補充說明 3：及物動詞、介詞之後的代詞一律用賓格，並列賓語亦是如此。

The objective case is correct in the following examples.

在以下的例句中，賓格的使用是正確的。

例如：

The ranger offered Shirley and him some advice on campsites.【護林員向雪莉和他提供了一些關於露營地的建議。】

They came to meet the Baldwins and us.【他們來見鮑德溫一家和我們。】

Let's talk it over between us, then, you and me. 【讓我們談談吧，你和我。】

Whom should I ask? 【我應該問誰？】

A group of us taxpayers protested. 【我們一群納稅人抗議了。】

Us in the last example is in apposition to taxpayers, the object of the preposition of. The wording, although grammatically defensible, is rarely apt. "A group of us protested as taxpayers" is better, if not exactly equivalent.

在最後一個例句中，us 是 taxpayers 的同位語，兩者一起作介詞 of 的賓語。這樣的用詞方式，雖然在文法上說得過去，但是不合乎常規使用習慣。改成「A group of us protested as taxpayers」，主格作主語，會更好，雖然與原義不完全一致。

補充說明 4：人稱代詞比反身代詞更適合做主語。

Use the simple personal pronoun as a subject.

用簡單的人稱代詞作主語。

例如：

Blake and myself stayed home.（✗）【布萊克和我自己待在家裡。】

Blake and I stayed home.（✓）【布萊克和我待在家裡。】

Howard and yourself brought the lunch, I thought. (✗)【霍華德和你自己帶了午餐，我想。】

Howard and you brought the lunch, I thought. (√)【霍華德和你帶了午餐，我想。】

補充說明 5：代詞的屬「格」或稱「所有格」。

The possessive case of pronouns is used to show ownership. It has two forms: the adjectival modifier, your hat, and the noun form, a hat of yours.

物主代詞是用來表示所屬關係的。分為兩種形式：形容詞性物主代詞 your hat 和名詞性物主代詞 a hat of yours。

例如：

The dog has buried one of your gloves and one of mine in the flower bed.【狗把你的一隻手套和我的一隻手套埋在花壇裡。】

補充說明 6：代詞格與非謂語動詞的搭配，分三個層次討論。

(1) 代詞所有格＋動名詞。

Gerunds usually require the possessive case.

動名詞前的代詞用形容詞性物主代詞形式。

例如：

Mother objected to our driving on the icy roads.【媽媽反對我們在結冰的路上開車。】

(2)代詞賓格＋現在分詞。

A present participle as a verbal, on the other hand, takes the objective case.

現在分詞前的代詞要用賓格。

例如：

They heard him singing in the shower.【他們聽到他在洗澡時唱歌。】

(3)現在分詞與動名詞的區別。

The difference between a verbal participle and a gerund is not always obvious, but note what is really said in each of the following.

現在分詞和動名詞之間的區分不總是明確的，注意以下例句的含義有什麼分別。

例如：

Do you mind me asking a question?【你介意我問一個問題嗎？】

Do you mind my asking a question?【你介意我問的一個問題嗎？】

In the first sentence, the queried objection is to me, as opposed to other members of the group, asking a question. In the second example, the issue is whether a question may be asked at all.

在第一個例句中,重點在賓語 me,是指相對其他人,「我」能不能問一個問題;在第二個例句中,my 成了 asking 的修飾成分,重點在 asking,只是在說能不能問問題了。

1-11　邏輯主語

Rule 11　A participial phrase at the beginning of a sentence must refer to the grammatical subject

規則十一　位於句首的分詞片語,要與主句的主語相關

例如:

Walking slowly down the road, he saw a woman accompanied by two children. 【他在路上慢慢地走時,看到一個女人帶著兩個孩子。】

The word walking refers to the subject of the sentence, not to the woman. To make it refer to the woman, the writer must recast the sentence.

walking 一詞的邏輯主語,是主句主語 he,而不是 woman。如果 walking 的主語要是 woman,作者須要把句子改寫如下:

He saw a woman, accompanied by two children, walking slowly down the road. 【他看見一個女人,帶著兩個孩子,慢慢地走在路上。】

補充說明:相關就近的原則,適用於多種游離於主句之外的結構。

Participial phrases preceded by a conjunction or by a preposition, nouns in apposition, adjectives, and adjective phrases come under the same rule if they begin the sentence.

連詞或介詞＋分詞結構、作為同位語的名詞、形容詞和形容詞片語,位於主句之前時,也要遵循這條規則。

例如:

On arriving in Chicago, his friends met him at the station.(✗)【他抵達芝加哥後,他的朋友們在車站迎接他。】

On arriving in Chicago, he was met at the station by his friends.(√)【他抵達芝加哥後,在車站受到朋友們的迎接。】

Part 1　運用與組合規則

A soldier of proved valor, they entrusted him with the defense of the city.（✗）【作為一名英勇的士兵，他們委託他保衛城市。】

A soldier of proved valor, he was entrusted with the defense of the city.（✓）【作為一名英勇的士兵，他被委託保衛城市。】

Young and inexperienced, the task seemed easy to me.（✗）【年輕且缺乏經驗，這項任務對我來說似乎很容易。】

Young and inexperienced, I thought the task easy.（✓）【年輕而缺乏經驗，使我認為這項任務很容易。】

Without a friend to counsel him, the temptation proved irresistible.（✗）【沒有朋友為他提供建議，這種誘惑被證明是不可抗拒的。】

Without a friend to counsel him, he found the temptation irresistible.（✓）【在沒有朋友為他提供建議的情況下，他發現這種誘惑無法抗拒。】

Sentences violating Rule 11 are often ludicrous.
違背規則 11 寫出的句子經常是荒謬可笑的。

例如：

Being in a dilapidated condition, I was able to buy the house very cheap.【在破舊的情況下，我能夠以非常便宜的價格買到房子。】

Wondering irresolutely what to do next, the clock struck twelve.
【猶豫不決地想下一步該做什麼，時鐘敲響了十二點。】

2-1　文章格局構思

Rule 12　Choose a suitable design and hold to it
規則十二　選擇適合的結構設定並保持不變

A basic structural design underlies every kind of writing. Writers will in part follow this design, in part deviate from it, according to their skills, their needs, and the unexpected events that accompany the act of composition. Writing, to be effective, must follow closely the thoughts of the writer, but not necessarily in the order in which those thoughts occur. This calls for a scheme of procedure. In some cases, the best design is no design, as with a love letter, which is simply an outpouring, or with a casual essay, which is a ramble. But in most cases, planning must be a deliberate prelude to writing. The first principle of composition, therefore, is to foresee or determine the shape of what is to come and pursue that shape.

Part 1　運用與組合規則

　　一個基本結構設定是每種寫作的基礎。作者一方面遵循這種設定，一方面又會偏離，這取決於他們的寫作技巧、寫作需求，以及寫作中的意外內容。好的寫作，必須緊隨作者的思想，但不必按照思想產生的先後順序。這就要求在寫作前先構思。在有些情況下，最好的構思就是沒有構思，就像情書，就是單純的情感流露，或者散文隨筆，就是漫談。但是在大多數情況下，寫作之前還是要有一個周密計畫。因此，寫作的首要原則，就是預先構想或確定一種文章格局，並遵從這種格局寫作。

A sonnet is built on a fourteen-line frame, each line containing five feet. Hence, sonneteers know exactly where they are headed, although they may not know how to get there. Most forms of composition are less clearly defined, more flexible, but all have skeletons to which the writer will bring the flesh and the blood. The more clearly the writer perceives the shape, the better are the chances of success.

　　十四行詩由十四行詩句組成，每一行包括五個音步。因此，十四行詩的作者一開始明確知道作品會寫成什麼樣子，儘管他也許還不知道具體怎麼寫。大多數文體都沒有這麼固定的框架，都更靈活，但是都必須要有一個骨架，以便作者能將血肉填充進去。格局框架越清楚，作者成功的機會越大。

2-2　文章的分段

Rule 13　Make the paragraph the unit of composition: one paragraph to each topic

規則十三　文章要以段落為單位：每段有一個獨立主題

拆分為 8 個小問題來討論：

問題 1 同一段落的句子要保持統一、連貫。

The paragraph is a convenient unit; it serves all forms of literary work. As long as it holds together, a paragraph may be of any length— a single, short sentence or a passage of great duration.

段落是一種比較好用的單位；它適用於一切文章形式。只要能連貫，一個段落可長可短 —— 一句或多句皆可。

問題 2 主題可以拆分成若干分論點。

If the subject on which you are writing is of slight extent, or if you intend to treat it briefly, there may be no need to divide it into topics.

如果你的寫作的主題涉及面不大，或者你打算簡要闡述，就沒有必要拆分成幾個分論點。

※ 提示：全文主題是 subject，各段分論點是 topic。

Thus, a brief description, a brief book review, a brief account of a single incident, a narrative merely outlining an action, the setting forth of a single idea— any one of these is best written in a single paragraph. After the paragraph has been written, examine it to see whether division will improve it. Ordinarily, however, a subject requires division into topics, each of which should be dealt with in a paragraph. The object of treating each topic in a paragraph by itself is, of course, to aid the reader.

因此，簡短描述、簡要書評、事件概述、行動概要、理念簡介──以上這些最好都寫成一段。完成後，再來推敲拆成幾段是否會更好。然而一般來講，一個主題還是要拆分成幾個分論點，每一個分論點作為一段。而把每個分論點作為一段的目的，當然是為了方便讀者閱讀。

問題 3 主題句放在段落的開頭。

The beginning of each paragraph is a signal that a new step in the development of the subject has been reached. As a rule, single sentences should not be written or printed as paragraphs. An exception may be made of sentences of transition, indicating the relation between the parts of an exposition or argument.

2-2 文章的分段

　　每段的開頭部分,最好是一個標明主題推進到了新階段的訊號。按常規,一個句子不應該單獨成段。但在說明或議論中,表明上下段關係的過渡句,可以例外。

問題 4 對話中,每個人的話另起一段寫。

　　In dialogue, each speech, even if only a single word, is usually a paragraph by itself; that is, a new paragraph begins with each change of speaker. The application of this rule when dialogue and narrative are combined is best learned from examples in well-edited works of fiction. Sometimes a writer, seeking to create an effect of rapid talk or for some other reason, will elect not to set off each speech in a separate paragraph and instead will run speeches together. The common practice, however, and the one that serves best in most instances, is to give each speech a paragraph of its own.

　　在對話中,每個人說的話,即使只有一個詞,通常也要自成一段;也就是說,每換一個說話者,就要重啟一段。當敘述和對話內容摻雜出現時,這種規則的使用,最好從編輯好的小說案例中去學習。有時,為了某種原因,作者試圖營造一種對答如流的談話效果,會選擇不把每個人說的話單獨分段,而是寫在一起。然而一般來說,多數情境最適用的做法,還是每個人說的話各自成段。

問題 5 每個段落在文中的身分地位要明確。

As a rule, begin each paragraph either with a sentence that suggests the topic or with a sentence that helps the transition. If a paragraph forms part of a larger composition, its relation to what precedes, or its function as a part of the whole, may need to be expressed. This can sometimes be done by a mere word or phrase (again, therefore, for the same reason) in the first sentence. Sometimes, however, it is expedient to get into the topic slowly, by way of a sentence or two of introduction or transition.

按照常規，一段的開頭句，要麼用於提出分論點，要麼幫助過渡。作為更長的文章的一部分，一個段落與之前內容的關係，或是這個段落在整篇文章中發揮的功能，都需要交代清楚。有時，只需在段落首句新增一個詞（組）即可，如 again、therefore、for the same reason。但有時，最好還是透過一兩個引導性或過渡性的句子，緩慢進入分論點。

問題 6 段落開頭句與後面句子的關係。

In narration and description, the paragraph sometimes begins with a concise, comprehensive statement serving to hold together the details that follow.

在敘述和描寫中，有時以一個精簡、濃縮的表達，來整合隨後出現的細節。

2-2 文章的分段

例如：

The breeze served us admirably.【微風吹得我們很愜意。】

The campaign opened with a series of reverses.【競選活動以一系列逆轉開始。】

The next ten or twelve pages were filled with a curious set of entries.【接下來的十到十二頁充滿了一系列奇怪的條目。】

But when this device, or any device, is too often used, it becomes a mannerism. More commonly, the opening sentence simply indicates by its subject the direction the paragraph is to take.

但是這種手段，或任何手段，過於頻繁地使用，都會顯得做作。更為常見的做法是，僅僅用段落首句簡要表明本段主題的推進方向就可以了。

例如：

At length I thought I might return toward the stockade.【最終，我想我可能會回到寨子。】

He picked up the heavy lamp from the table and began to explore.【他從桌上拿起沉重的檯燈，開始研究。】

Another flight of steps, and they emerged on the roof.【又走了一段臺階後，他們來到了屋頂。】

Part 1　運用與組合規則

問題 7 短小段落的劃分是為了修辭效果。

In animated narrative, the paragraphs are likely to be short and without any semblance of a topic sentence, the writer rushing headlong, event following event in rapid succession. The break between such paragraphs merely serves the purpose of a rhetorical pause, throwing into prominence some detail of the action.

在生動型敘述中，段落可能短小，沒有任何類似分論點的句子，作者寫得快速直接，事件接踵而至。這種分段不過是為了修辭上停頓的需求，突出故事的某些細節。

問題 8 分段是為了從形式到邏輯都方便讀者閱讀。

In general, remember that paragraphing calls for a good eye as well as a logical mind. Enormous blocks of print look formidable to readers, who are often reluctant to tackle them. Therefore, breaking long paragraphs in two, even if it is not necessary to do so for sense, meaning, or logical development, is often a visual help.

要記住，一般來講，分段要求賞心悅目同時邏輯合理。大段大段的文字，會令讀者望而生畏，所以他們常不願去讀。因此，把很長的段落一分為二，即使在表意和邏輯推衍上未必必要，但是在視覺效果上常有幫助。

But remember, too, that firing off many short paragraphs in quick succession can be distracting. Paragraph breaks used only for show read like the writing of commerce or of display advertising. Moderation and a sense of order should be the main considerations in paragraphing.

但是也要記住，一連寫出許多小段落，也容易讓人分心。只為視覺效果而分段，讀起來就會像是流水帳或廣告牌。合理有序應該是分段的主要考量。

2-3　使用主動語態

Rule14　Use the active voice
規則十四　要用主動語態

The active voice is usually more direct and vigorous than the passive.

主動語態通常比被動語態更直接有力。

例如：

I shall always remember my first visit to Boston.【我將永遠記得我第一次訪問波士頓。】

This is much better than 要優於：

Part 1　運用與組合規則

My first visit to Boston will always be remembered by me.【我的第一次訪問波士頓將永遠被我記住。】

The latter sentence is less direct, less bold, and less concise. If the writer tries to make it more concise by omitting "by me", it becomes indefinite:

後一個句子不如前一個直接、鮮明、簡潔。而如果作者為了簡潔，刪除「by me」，句子將變得不明確：

My first visit to Boston will always be remembered.【我第一次訪問波士頓將永遠被記住。】

Is it the writer or some undisclosed person or the world at large that will always remember this visit?

將永遠記住波士頓之行的，是作者，是未知的某人，還是世界上所有人？

This rule does not, of course, mean that the writer should entirely discard the passive voice, which is frequently convenient and sometimes necessary.

當然，這條規則不是說作者應該完全拋棄被動語態，使用被動語態經常也是方便的，有時甚至是必要的。

例如：

The dramatists of the Restoration are little esteemed today.【英王復辟時期的劇作家如今很少受到尊重。】

2-3 使用主動語態

Modern readers have little esteem for the dramatists of the Restoration. 【如今的讀者對英王復辟時期的劇作家少有尊重。】

The first would be the preferred form in a paragraph on the dramatists of the Restoration, the second in a paragraph on the tastes of modern readers. The need to make a particular word the subject of the sentence will often, as in these examples, determine which voice is to be used.

前一個例句適於「英王復辟時期劇作家」作為話題的文段，後一個適於「現代讀者閱讀品味」作為話題的文段。正如這兩個例句所示，文章需要哪個特定的詞來作為句子的主語，常常決定了句子用主動還是被動語態。

補充說明：

The habitual use of the active voice, however, makes for forcible writing. This is true not only in narrative concerned principally with action but in writing of any kind. Many a tame sentence of description or exposition can be made lively and emphatic by substituting a transitive in the active voice for some such perfunctory expression as there is or could be heard.

然而習慣上，使用主動語態，可以使寫作更有力量。不僅對於描述情節的記敘文如此，任何文體都如此。在描述或說明中，透過替換主動形態的及物動詞諸如「there is」、「could be heard」這類敷衍的表述，很多平淡的句子就能夠變得鮮活、有力。

Part 1　運用與組合規則

例如：

比較下面左邊和右邊的句子，右邊的句子明顯優於左邊：

There was a great number of dead leaves lying on the ground.（✗）【地上散落著大量枯葉。】

Dead leaves covered the ground.（√）【枯葉鋪滿地面。】

At dawn the crowing of a rooster could be heard.（✗）【黎明時分，公雞的叫聲可以被聽到。】

The cock's crow came with dawn.（√）【公雞的叫聲伴隨著黎明而來。】

The reason he left college was that his health became impaired.（✗）【他離開大學的原因是他的健康受損。】

Failing health compelled him to leave college.（√）【健康不佳迫使他離開大學。】

It was not long before she was very sorry that she had said what she had.（✗）【沒過多久，她就很抱歉她說了那些話。】

She soon repented her words.（√）【很快，她就後悔說了那些話。】

Note, in the examples above, that when a sentence is made stronger, it usually becomes shorter. Thus, brevity is a by-product of vigor.

注意，在以上的例子中，通常句子越簡潔就越強而有力。因此也可以說，簡潔與活力共生。

提示：其實在講述同一件事的時候，使用不同的動詞，敘述的角度加以變化，事物和人都可以做主語，有助於在主被動語態間靈活切換。

2-4　使用肯定式

Rule 15　Put statements in positive form
規則十五　要用肯定的表達

Make definite assertions. Avoid tame, colorless, hesitating, noncommittal language. Use the word not as a means of denial or in antithesis, never as a means of evasion.

觀點要明確。避開平淡、無味、猶豫、曖昧的語言。not 是用於否定、反駁的，而絕不是迴避的手段。

例如：

He was not very often on time. (✗) 【他不經常準時。】

He usually came late. (✓) 【他經常遲到。】

She did not think that studying Latin was a sensible way to use one's time. (✗) 【她不認為學習拉丁語是一種合理利用時間的方式。】

She thought the study of Latin a waste of time. (✓) 【她認為學習拉丁語是在浪費時間。】

The Taming of the Shrew is rather weak in spots. Shakespeare does not portray Katharine as a very admirable character, nor does Bianca remain long in memory as an important character in Shakespeare's works. (✗) 【《馴悍記》在某些方面相當薄弱。莎士比亞沒把凱薩琳描繪成一個非常令人欽佩的角色，比安卡也沒有作為莎士比亞作品的重要角色而長存於人們的記憶。】

The women in *The Taming of the Shrew* are unattractive. Katharine is disagreeable, Bianca insignificant. (✓) 【《馴悍記》中的女人沒有吸引力。凱薩琳令人討厭，比安卡無足輕重。】

2-4　使用肯定式

The last example, before correction, is indefinite as well as negative. The corrected version, consequently, is simply a guess at the writer's intention.

最後一個例句，修改前的版本，是從反面的表達，不夠明確。修改後的結果，只是對作者意圖的猜測。

All three examples show the weakness inherent in the word not. Consciously or unconsciously, the reader is dissatisfied with being told only what is not; the reader wishes to be told what is. Hence, as a rule, it is better to express even a negative in positive form.

三個例句都表明了「not」這個詞的本質弱點。無論自覺與否，讀者對於否定的表達都是不滿意的；讀者想要肯定的表述。因此，即使是負面資訊，也要用肯定的方式表達，效果更好。

例如：

not honest 【不誠實】 —— dishonest 【虛偽】

not important 【不重要】 —— trifling 【次要】

did not remember 【不記得】 —— forgot 【忘記】

did not pay any attention to 【沒注意】 —— ignored 【忽視】

did not have much confidence in 【不信】 —— distrusted 【懷疑】

Part 1　運用與組合規則

補充說明 1：肯定否定對比結構。

Placing negative and positive in opposition makes for a stronger structure.

把肯定和否定的表達放在一起相互對比，會形成更強而有力的結構。

例如：

Not charity, but simple justice.【不是慈善，只是正義。】

Not that I loved Caesar less, but that I loved Rome more.【不是我不愛凱撒，而是我更愛羅馬。】

Ask not what your country can do for you — ask what you can do for your country.【不要問你的國家能為你做什麼——而要問你能為你的國家做什麼。】

補充說明 2：其他否定詞。

Negative words other than not are usually strong.

not 之外的其他否定詞通常有很強表達力。

例如：

Her loveliness I never knew / until she smiled on me.【我從不知道她的可愛／直到她對我微笑。】

補充說明 3：語氣助動詞。

Statements qualified with unnecessary auxiliaries or conditionals sound irresolute.

2-4 使用肯定式

搭配不必要的助動詞或條件從句的表達顯得不確定。

例如：

If you would let us know the time of your arrival, we would be happy to arrange your transportation from the airport.（✗）【如果您能告知您的抵達時間，我們就可能很樂意安排車子到機場來接您。】

If you will let us know the time of your arrival, we shall be happy to arrange your transportation from the airport.（✓）【如果您能告知您的抵達時間，我們將很樂意安排車子到機場來接您。】

Applicants can make a good impression by being neat and punctual.（✗）【申請人可能憑整潔和準時給人留下良好印象。】

Applicants will make a good impression if they are neat and punctual.（✓）【整潔、守時的應徵者會給人留下好印象。】

Plath may be ranked among those modern poets who died young.（✗）【普拉斯可能屬於那些英年早逝的現代詩人。】

Plath was one of those modern poets who died young.（✓）【普拉斯是一位英年早逝的現代詩人。】

If your every sentence admits a doubt, your writing will lack authority. Save the auxiliaries would, should, could, may, might, and can for situations involving real uncertainty.

如果你的每個句子都存疑，你的文章就會缺乏說服力。除非真的不確定，否則不要使用 would、should、could、may、might 和 can。

2-5 表達明確具體

Rule 16　Use definite, specific, concrete language
規則十六　使用明確、詳細、具體的語言

Prefer the specific to the general, the definite to the vague, the concrete to the abstract.

詳細比概括好，明確比模糊好，具體比抽象好。

例如：

A period of unfavorable weather set in. (✗)【一段不討喜的天氣開始了。】

It rained every day for a week. (✓)【連續一週每天都下雨。】

2-5 表達明確具體

He showed satisfaction as he took possession of his well-earned reward.（✗）【當得到他來之不易的獎賞時，他表現出滿足。】

He grinned as he pocketed the coin.（√）【他咧嘴笑著把錢幣裝進口袋。】

If those who have studied the art of writing are in accord on any one point, it is this: the surest way to arouse and hold the reader's attention is by being specific, definite, and concrete. The greatest writers, Homer, Dante, Shakespeare, are effective largely because they deal in particulars and report the details that matter. Their words call up pictures.

研究過寫作藝術的人一致同意：引起並保持讀者注意力最切實有效的方法，就是詳細、明確和具體。最偉大的作家們——荷馬、但丁、莎士比亞的成功相當程度上就在於他們講述個體，交代重要細節。他們的語言具有畫面感。

Jean Stafford, to cite a more modern author, demonstrates in her short story "*In the Zoo*" how prose is made vivid by the use of words that evoke images and sensations:

以現代作家珍‧斯塔福的小說《在動物園裡》為例，我們來看看她如何用形象、具體的詞彙使散文變得生動活潑。

Part 1　運用與組合規則

... Daisy and I in time found asylum in a small menagerie down by the railroad tracks. It belonged to a gentle alcoholic ne'er-do-well, who did nothing all day long but drink bathtub gin in rickeys and play solitaire and smile to himself and talk to his animals. He had a little, stunted red vixen and a deodorized skunk, a parrot from Tahiti that spoke Parisian French, a woebegone coyote, and two capuchin monkeys, so serious and humanized, so small and sad and sweet, and so religious-looking with their tonsured heads that it was impossible not to think their gibberish was really an ordered language with a grammar that someday some philologist would understand.【……黛西和我及時在鐵路旁的一個小動物園裡找到了避難所。動物園屬於一個溫和的酒鬼，他整天無所事事，只是痛飲利克酒和琴酒，玩紙牌遊戲，對自己發笑，跟他的動物們說話。他有一隻發育不良的小紅狐狸和一隻除臭臭鼬、一隻來自大溪地的會說巴黎法語的鸚鵡、一隻憂傷的郊狼，還有兩隻捲尾猴，表情嚴肅，通人性，矮小、憂傷而可親，頭髮剃得精光，一副虔誠的樣子。因此人們肯定會以為，他們的胡言亂語其實是一種有序、有規律的語言，總有一天某位文法學家能搞懂。】

Gran knew about our visits to Mr. Murphy and she did not object, for it gave her keen pleasure to excoriate him when we came home. His vice was not a matter of guesswork; it was an established fact that he was half-seas over from dawn till midnight. "With the black Irish," said Gran, "the taste for drink is taken in with the mother's milk and is never mastered. Oh, I know all about those promises to join the temperance movement and not to touch another drop. The way to Hell is paved with good intentions."【格蘭知道我們拜訪墨菲先生的事,她沒有反對,因為當我們回到家後,她可以痛痛快快地罵他一頓。他的惡習可是確鑿的事實:一天到晚喝得半醉半醒。「愛爾蘭皮膚黝黑的人,」格蘭說,「吃奶的以後就會喝酒了,一生都不會節制。噢,至於什麼參加禁酒運動以後滴酒不沾的諾言,我可是聽膩了。準備下地獄還說是好意呢。」】

If the experiences of Walter Mitty, of Molly Bloom, of Rabbit Angstrom have seemed for the moment real to countless readers, if in reading Faulkner we have almost the sense of inhabiting Yoknapatawpha County during the decline of the South, it is because the details used are definite, the terms concrete. It is not that every detail is given—that would be impossible, as well as to no purpose—but that all the significant details are given, and with such accuracy and vigor that readers, in imagination, can project themselves into the scene.

如果華特・米蒂(Walter Mitty)、莫莉・布魯(Molly Bloom)和兔子四部曲(Rabbit Angstrom)的經歷讓無數讀者感

Part 1　運用與組合規則

覺身臨其境，那麼閱讀福克納作品，讓我們感覺就如同在美國南部衰落時期，居住在約克納帕塔瓦帕（Yoknapatawpha）郡一樣，這是因為其中細節明確，語言具體。不是作者描述了每一個細節――那是不可能也沒有必要的――而是所有重要細節都得以呈現，並且這些細節如此準確生動，以至於，讀者能夠在想像中身臨其境。

In exposition and in argument, the writer must likewise never lose hold of the concrete; and even when dealing with general principles, the writer must furnish particular instances of their application.

同樣，在說明文和議論文中，作者也必須牢牢把握具體案例；即使在論證大原則時，也必須提供具體例子。

In his *Philosophy of Style*, Herbert Spencer gives two sentences to illustrate how the vague and general can be turned into the vivid and particular:

赫伯特・史賓賽在他的《文體哲學》中給出了兩個例子，說明如何把模糊籠統的句子改得生動具體：

| In proportion as the manners, customs, and amusements of a nation are cruel and barbarous, the regulations of | In proportion as men delight in battles, bullfights, and combats of gladiators, will they punish by hanging, burn- |

its penal code will be severe. (✗)【一個國家的禮儀、風俗和娛樂越是殘酷和野蠻,其刑法規定就越嚴厲。】

ing, and the rack.(√)【人們越喜歡戰鬥、鬥牛和角鬥,就越會用絞刑、焚燒和撕拉肢體的刑法。】

To show what happens when strong writing is deprived of its vigor, George Orwell once took a passage from the *Bible* and drained it of its blood. On the left, below, is Orwell's translation; on the right, the verse from *Ecclesiastes* (King James Version).

喬治・奧威爾(George Orwell)曾節選了《聖經》中的一章,去其血肉,來展示那些極富表現力的文字被剝奪了生機之後是什麼樣子。以下是喬治・奧威爾(George Orwell)處理後的譯文,右邊是《傳道書》(英文欽定版)的原句。

Objective consideration of contemporary phenomena compels the conclusion that success or failure in competitive activities exhibits no tendency to be commensurate with innate capacity, but that a considerable element of the unpredictable must inevitably be

I returned, and saw under the sun, that the race is not to the swift, nor the battle to the strong, neither yet bread to the wise, nor yet riches to men of understanding, nor yet favor to men of skill; but time and chance happeneth to them all.(√)【轉念間,我看

taken into account.（✗）【客觀考察當代現象，必然得出這樣的結論：競爭中的成敗與天賦無關，倒是一種不可預測的因素必須要考慮。】

到在陽光下，賽跑不青睞快的人，戰鬥不偏袒強壯的人，智者未必富有，巧者未必飽腹，時機終對所有人均等。】

2-6 刪除不必要的詞

Rule 17 Omit needless words
規則十七　刪除不必要的詞語

Vigorous writing is concise. A sentence should contain no unnecessary words, a paragraph no unnecessary sentences, for the same reason that a drawing should have no unnecessary lines and a machine no unnecessary parts. This requires not that the writer make all sentences short, or avoid all detail and treat subjects only in outline, but that every word tells.

有生命力的作品是精簡的。一個句子中不應有多餘的詞，一個段落中不應有多餘的句，就像一幅畫中不應有多餘的線條，一部機器不應有多餘的零件一樣。這不是說，作者

2-6 刪除不必要的詞

只能寫短句子，或要避開所有細節，僅僅把主題勾勒出大致輪廓，而是說，每個詞都必須有資訊量。

Many expressions in common use violate this principle.

然而許多常用表達都違背了這條原則。

例如：

八種寫作中習以為常但囉唆的片語：

the question as to whether ➡ whether (the question whether)

there is no doubt but that ➡ no doubt (doubtless)

used for fuel purposes ➡ used for fuel he is a man who ➡ he in a hasty manner ➡ hastily this is a subject that ➡ this subject

Her story is a strange one. ➡ Her story is strange.

the reason why is that ➡ because

補充說明 1：常見的空洞抽象詞包括：fact / case 事實；character / nature 性質。

"The fact that" is an especially debilitating expression. It should be revised out of every sentence in which it occurs.

The fact that 「事實是」這個表達特別無力，應該從所有句子中刪除。

例如：

owing to the fact that ➡ since (because)

in spite of the fact that ➡ though (although)

call your attention to the fact that ➡ remind you (notify you)

I was unaware of the fact that ➡ I was unaware that (did not know)

the fact that he had not succeeded ➡ his failure the fact that I had arrived ➡ my arrival

See also the words case, character, nature in Chapter IV. Who is, which was, and the like are often superfluous.

此外，還有第四部分中將說到的 case、character、nature 等詞也與 fact 同理。who is、which was 一類結構也常是多餘的。

例如：

his cousin, who is a member of the same firm （✗）【他的表弟，是同一家公司成員的某人】

his cousin, a member of the same firm （√）【他的表弟，同一家公司的成員】

Trafalgar, which was Nelson's last battle （✗）【特拉法加，這是尼爾森的最後一戰】

Trafalgar, Nelson's last battle （√）【特拉法加，尼爾森的最後一戰】

2-6 刪除不必要的詞

As the active voice is more concise than the passive, and a positive statement more concise than a negative one, many of the examples given under Rule 14 and Rule 15 illustrate this rule as well.

由於主動語態比被動語態簡明、肯定表達比否定表達簡明，所以規則十四和十五中的很多例句也適用本規則。

補充說明2：減少句子的數量。

A common way to fall into wordiness is to present a single complex idea, step by step, in a series of sentences that might to advantage be combined into one.

一種常見的濫用詞藻的方式，是用一系列的句子，一步一步地表達一個複雜的觀點，而更好的做法是將之合成一個句子。

例如：

Macbeth was very ambitious. 【馬克白雄心勃勃。】

This led him to wish to become king of Scotland. 【這致使他希望成為蘇格蘭國王。】

The witches told him that this wish of his would come true. 【女巫告訴他，他的這個願望會實現。】

The king of Scotland at this time was Duncan. 【此時的蘇格蘭國王是鄧肯。】

Encouraged by his wife, Macbeth murdered Duncan. 【在妻子的鼓勵下，馬克白謀殺了鄧肯。】

He was thus enabled to succeed Duncan as king. 【他因此能夠接替鄧肯成為國王。】

（以上六個短句合計 51 個詞）

Encouraged by his wife, Macbeth achieved his ambition and realized the prediction of the witches by murdering Duncan and becoming king of Scotland in his place. 【在妻子的鼓勵下，馬克白實現了自己的野心，實現了女巫的預言，殺死了鄧肯，接替其位置成為蘇格蘭國王。】

（合併為一個長句後，只有 26 個詞）

2-7　重要資訊後置

Rule 18　Avoid a succession of loose sentences
規則十八　不要使用一連串結構鬆散的句子

This rule refers especially to loose sentences of a particular type: those consisting of two clauses, the second introduced by a conjunction or relative. A writer may err by making sentences too compact and periodic. An occasional loose sentence prevents the style from becoming too formal and gives the reader a certain relief. Consequently, loose sentences are common in easy, unstudied writing. The danger is that there may be too many of them.

這條規則專門針對一類特殊的鬆散句，即：包括兩個從句，且第二個從句由一個連詞或關係詞引出的情況。作者可能錯在把句子寫得太短小，且斷句太頻繁。偶爾使用鬆散句，可以避免文章顯得太過正式，使讀者得到某種放鬆。所以，鬆散句常用於簡單、非學術型的寫作。但過多使用這種句子則是危險的。

An unskilled writer will sometimes construct a whole paragraph of sentences of this kind, using as connectives and, but, and, less frequently, who, which, when, where, and while, these last in non-restrictive senses. (See Rule 3.)

技巧不夠嫻熟的作者有時會整段都寫這類句子，使用連詞 and、but，其次是用連詞 who、which、when、where、和 while 引導非限定性從句。（參見規則三。）

例如：以下兩段文字的優劣對比，前一段較差，後一段較好。

The third concert of the subscription series was given last evening, and a large audience was in attendance. Mr. Edward

Part 1　運用與組合規則

Appleton was the soloist, and the Boston Symphony Orchestra furnished the instrumental music. The former showed himself to be an artist of the first rank, while the latter proved itself fully deserving of its high reputation. The interest aroused by the series has been very gratifying to the Committee, and it is planned to give a similar series annually hereafter. The fourth concert will be given on Tuesday, May 10, when an equally attractive program will be presented.

【慈善音樂會第三場義演昨晚舉行，聽眾很多。愛德華・艾普頓先生獨奏，波士頓交響樂隊表演了器樂。前者展示了一流的技藝，後者實至名歸。組織方很滿意音樂會引起了公眾興趣，並計劃今後每年都要舉辦類似的義演。第四場義演將於 5 月 10 日星期二舉行，屆時將演出同樣高品質的節目。】

Apart from its triteness and emptiness, the paragraph above is bad because of the structure of its sentences, with their mechanical symmetry and singsong. Compare these sentences from the chapter "What I Believe" in E. M. Forster's *Two Cheers for Democracy*:

以上這段文字之所以糟糕，除了陳腐、空洞以外，還在於其句子結構機械對稱、節奏單調。與之比較，再來看以下

2-7 重要資訊後置

這段來自 E·M· 福斯特《為民主再喝采》的「我的信仰」一章中的句子：

I believe in aristocracy, though — if that is the right word, and if a democrat may use it. Not an aristocracy of power, based upon rank and influence, but an aristocracy of the sensitive, the considerate and the plucky. Its members are to be found in all nations and classes, and all through the ages, and there is a secret understanding between them when they meet. They represent the true human tradition, the one permanent victory of our queer race over cruelty and chaos. Thousands of them perish in obscurity, a few are great names. They are sensitive to others as well as for themselves, they are considerate without being fussy, their pluck is not swankiness but the power to endure, and they can take a joke.【不過，我信仰貴族政治 —— 如果這是一個正確的詞，如果民主黨人可以使用的話。不是基於階級和影響力的當權貴族，而是敏感、體貼、勇敢的貴族政治。其成員遍布各個民族、階級和年齡層，他們相遇時彼此有一種默契。他們代表著真正的人類傳統，極少數人對抗殘酷和混亂，並得到持久的勝利。他們中成千上萬的人在默默無聞中逝去，少數一些得以流芳百世。他們對別人和對自己同樣地通情達理，他們體貼周到，從不大驚小怪，他們的勇敢不是張揚炫耀，而是堅毅隱忍，而且他們也會輕鬆說笑。】

Part 1　運用與組合規則

A writer who has written a series of loose sentences should recast enough of them to remove the monotony, replacing them with simple sentences, sentences of two clauses joined by a semicolon, periodic sentences of two clauses, or sentences (loose or periodic) of three clauses— whichever best represent the real relations of the thought.

一個寫了大量鬆散句的作者應該修改足夠多的內容，以避免單調乏味。改為幾個單句、分號連線的兩個並列句、包含兩個從句的圓周句，或者包含三個從句的圓周句或鬆散句──也就是，最能寫出作者真實思通行證理的任何句子構成方式。

2-8　內容決定句型

Rule 19　Express coordinate ideas in similar form
規則十九　要用類似的形式表達並列的意思

This principle, that of parallel construction, requires that expressions similar in content and function be outwardly similar. The likeness of form enables the reader to recognize more readily the likeness of content and function. The familiar Beatitudes exemplify the virtue of parallel construction.

這條平行結構原則，要求內容、功能相似的表達要有相似的形式。表達形式的相似能讓讀者更容易辨識內容和功能的相似。為人所熟悉的福音書中的句子就是平行結構的優秀典範。

例如：

Blessed are the poor in spirit: for theirs is the kingdom of heaven.【虛心者有福了：因為他們所擁有的是天國。】

Blessed are they that mourn: for they shall be comforted.【哀慟者有福了：因為他們將獲得安慰。】

Blessed are the meek: for they shall inherit the earth.【溫順者有福了：因為他們將繼承土地。】

Blessed are they which do hunger and thirst after righteousness: for they shall be filled.【逐義者有福了：因為他們將被滿足。】

The unskilled writer often violates this principle, mistakenly believing in the value of constantly varying the form of expression. When repeating a statement to emphasize it, the writer may need to vary its form. Otherwise, the writer should follow the principle of parallel construction.

技巧不嫻熟的作者常會違背此原則，錯誤地相信頻繁變換句式價值。當重複一個表達以表示強調時，作者也許需要變換形式。但除此以外，作者都應該遵從平行結構原則。

例如：

Formerly, science was taught by the textbook method, while now the laboratory method is employed.（✗）【以前科學是透過書本方法來教授，現在實驗教學方法被採用了。】

Formerly, science was taught by the textbook method; now it is taught by the laboratory method.（✓）【以前，科學透過書本教授；現在透過實驗。】

The left-hand version gives the impression that the writer is undecided or timid, apparently unable or afraid to choose one form of expression and hold to it. The righthand version shows that the writer has at least made a choice and abided by it.

以上例子中，左邊版本給人的印象是作者猶豫不決、戰戰兢兢，明顯不能或害怕選定一種表達形式並堅持到底。右邊版本則顯示出作者至少已經做出了一個決定並堅守了它。

補充說明 1：冠詞和介詞的平行

By this principle, an article or a preposition applying to all the members of a series must either be used only before the first term or else be repeated before each term.

依據本原則,適用於一個片語中所有單字的某冠詞或介詞,必須要麼只放在第一個單字前,要麼每個單字前都要放。

例如:

the French, Italians, Spanish, and Portuguese 【法國人、義大利人、西班牙人和葡萄牙人】

the French, the Italians, the Spanish, and the Portuguese 【法國人、義大利人、西班牙人和葡萄牙人】

in spring, summer, or in winter 【在春季、夏季或冬季】

in spring, summer, or winter 【在春季、夏季或冬季】

(in spring, in summer, or in winter) 【(在春季、夏季或冬季)】

Some words require a particular preposition in certain idiomatic uses. When such words are joined in a compound construction, all the appropriate prepositions must be included, unless they are the same.

一些單字在某些搭配中要求用特定的介詞。當這一類的單字出現在複合結構中時,這些特定介詞也必須寫出來,除非與其他介詞重複。

例如：

His speech was marked by disagreement and scorn for his opponent's position. (✗)【他的講話以不同意和蔑視對手的立場為特徵。】

His speech was marked by disagreement with and scorn for his opponent's position. (✓)【他的講話充滿了對對手立場的不同意和蔑視。】

補充說明 2：連詞的平行

Correlative expressions (both, and; not, but; not only, but also; either, or; first, second, third; and the like) should be followed by the same grammatical construction. Many violations of this rule can be corrected by rearranging the sentence.

both, and; not, but; not only, but also; either, or; first, second, third; and the like 等連線的關聯表達也要求有相似的文法結構。許多違背這條規則的表達都能透過重新安排句子結構予以修正。

例如：

It was both a long ceremony and very tedious. (✗)【這既是一個漫長的儀式，也很乏味。】

The ceremony was both long and tedious. (✓)【儀式既漫長又乏味。】

2-8 內容決定句型

A time not for words but action.（✗）【不是言語而是行動的時代。】

A time not for words but for action.（✓）【不是言語而是行動的時代。】

Either you must grant his request or incur his ill will.（✗）【要麼你必須同意他的請求，或招致他的惡意。】

You must either grant his request or incur his ill will.（✓）【你必然要麼同意他的請求，要麼招致他的惡意。】

My objections are, first, the injustice of the measure; second, that it is unconstitutional.（✗）【我的反對意見是，首先，措施的不公正，第二，它違憲。】

My objections are, first, that the measure is unjust; second, that it is unconstitutional.（✓）【我的反對意見是，首先，措施不公正，第二，它違憲。】

It may be asked, what if you need to express a rather large number of similar ideas — say, twenty? Must you write twenty consecutive sentences of the same pattern? On closer examination, you will probably find that the difficulty is imaginary — that these twenty ideas can be classified in groups, and that you need apply the principle only within each group. Otherwise, it is best to avoid the difficulty by putting statements in the form of a table.

Part 1　運用與組合規則

也許有人會問，如果你需要表達相當多（比方說 20 個）相似的想法時，又該如何呢？是否還是必須要寫成相似類型的 20 個連續的句子呢？細究起來，你可能會發現這樣的困難不過是想像出來的——即：這 20 個想法能夠分組，並僅在每組表達內部應用這一原則。然而，避免這種困難最好的辦法是把這些表達做成表格的形式。

2-9　相關詞放一起

Rule 20　Keep related words together
規則二十　要把相關的詞放在一起

The position of the words in a sentence is the principal means of showing their relationship. Confusion and ambiguity result when words are badly placed. The writer must, therefore, bring together the words and groups of words that are related in thought and keep apart those that are not so related.

單字在句子中的位置是展示詞語之間相互關係的最主要的方式。詞語的位置安排不當，會導致混亂和歧義。因此，作者必須把含義相關的詞和片語放到一起，不相關的隔離開。

2-9 相關詞放一起

例如：

He noticed a large stain in the rug that was right in the center.（✗）【他注意到在中央地毯有個大汙點。】

He noticed a large stain right in the center of the rug.（✓）【他注意到地毯中央有個大汙點。】

In the left-hand version of the first example, the reader has no way of knowing whether the stain was in the center of the rug or the rug was in the center of the room.

第一個例句，左邊的版本，讓讀者無從知道是汙點在地毯的中央，還是地毯在房間的中央。

You can call your mother in London and tell her all about George's taking you out to dinner for just two dollars.（✗）【你可以打電話給你在倫敦的媽媽，告訴她喬治帶你出去吃晚飯，只花兩美元。】

For just two dollars you can call your mother in London and tell her all about George's taking you out to dinner.（✓）【只要兩美元，你就可以打電話給你在倫敦的媽媽，告訴她喬治帶你出去吃晚飯。】

In the left-hand version of the second example, the reader may well wonder which cost two dollars — the phone call or the dinner.

089

Part 1　運用與組合規則

　　第二個例句，左邊的版本，讓讀者有足夠的理由疑惑：到底是電話還是晚餐花了 2 美元。

| New York's first commercial human-sperm bank opened Friday with semen samples from eighteen men frozen and stored in a stainless steel tank.（✗）【紐約第一家商業性質的人類精子庫於週五開業，有 18 個被冷凍並保存在不鏽鋼罐中的男性的精液樣本。】 | New York's first commercial human- sperm bank opened Friday when semen samples were taken from eighteen men. The samples were then frozen and stored in a stainless steel tank.（✓）【紐約第一家商業性質的人類精子庫於週五開業，當時採集了 18 名男性的精液樣本。然後將樣品冷凍並保存在不鏽鋼罐中。】 |

　　In the left-hand version of the third example, the reader's heart goes out to those eighteen poor fellows frozen in a steel tank.

　　第三個例句，左邊的版本，讓讀者極為關切被冷凍在不鏽鋼池子裡那 18 個可憐的傢伙。

補充說明 1：主語和謂語放在一起。

The subject of a sentence and the principal verb should not, as a rule, be separated by a phrase or clause that can be transferred to the beginning.

按規則，一個句子的主語與謂語核心動詞之間，不要插入一個片語或從句，這個片語和從句可以移動到句子開頭去。

例如：

Toni Morrison, in *Beloved*, writes about characters who have escaped from slavery but are haunted by its heritage. (✗)【托妮·莫里森，在《魅影情真》中，描寫了那些從奴隸制中逃脫但被奴隸制傳統困擾的人。】

In *Beloved*, Toni Morrison writes about characters who have escaped from slavery but are haunted by its heritage. (✓)【在《魅影情真》中，托妮·莫里森描寫了那些從奴隸制中逃脫但被奴隸制傳統困擾的人。】

A dog, if you fail to discipline him, becomes a household pest. (✗)【一條狗，如果你不管教牠，牠就會變成家裡的禍害。】

Unless disciplined, a dog becomes a household pest. (✓)【如果不加管教，一條狗會變成家裡的禍害。】

Interposing a phrase or a clause, as in the left-hand examples above, interrupts the flow of the main clause. This interruption, however, is not usually bothersome when the flow is checked only by a relative clause or by an expression in apposition. Sometimes, in periodic sentences, the interruption is a deliberate device for creating suspense. (See examples under Rule 22.)

在句子中間插入一個片語或從句，像以上例句左邊的版本那樣，會干擾主句的節奏。但是，如果插入的是關係從句或同位語，這種干擾通常就不那麼討厭了。有時候，在掉尾句中，這種干擾是為了設定懸念而有意為之。（參見規則二十二的例句。）

補充說明 2：先行詞和關係詞放在一起。

The relative pronoun should come, in most instances, immediately after its antecedent.

大多數情況下，關係代詞應該緊接在先行詞之後。

例如：

There was a stir in the audience that suggested disapproval. (✗) 【有一陣騷動在觀眾中表示不贊成。】

A stir that suggested disapproval swept the audience. (✓) 【一陣表示不贊成的騷動在觀眾中掀起。】

He wrote three articles about his adventures in Spain, which were published in *Harper's Magazine*.（✗）【他寫了三篇文章，關於他在西班牙的冒險經歷，發表在《哈潑雜誌》上。】

He published three articles in *Harper's Magazine* about his adventures in Spain.（✓）【他在《哈潑雜誌》上發表了三篇關於他在西班牙的冒險經歷的文章。】

This is a portrait of Benjamin Harrison, grandson of William Henry Harrison, who became President in 1889.（✗）【這是班傑明‧哈里森的肖像，威廉‧亨利‧哈里森的孫子，是1889年成為總統的。】

This is a portrait of Benjamin Harrison, who became President in 1889. He was the grandson of William Henry Harrison.（✓）【這是1889年成為總統的班傑明‧哈里森的肖像。他是威廉‧亨利‧哈里森的孫子。】

If the antecedent consists of a group of words, the relative comes at the end of the group, unless this would cause ambiguity.

如果先行詞是一個片語，在不造成歧義的情況下，關係詞應置於片語末尾。

Part 1 運用與組合規則

例如：

The Superintendent of the Chicago Division, who… 【芝加哥分部的負責人，他……】

No ambiguity results from the above. But 以上的例句不會產生歧義，但是，以下的例句就會使讀者疑惑，

"A proposal to amend the Sherman Act, which has been variously judged" 【「一項修改休曼法案的提案，經過不同的判斷」】

leaves the reader wondering whether it is the proposal or the Act that has been variously judged. The relative clause must be moved forward, to read,

被給予不同評價的是提議還是法案。這個關係從句必須被移動到前面，寫作，

"A proposal, which has been variously judged, to amend the Sherman Act..." 【「一項經過各種評判的提議，修改休曼法案……」】

Similarly 同樣地，

the grandson of William Henry Harrison, who（ ✗ ）【威廉‧亨利‧哈里森的孫子，他】

William Henry Harrison's grandson, Benjamin Harrison, who（ ✓ ）【威廉‧亨利‧哈里森的孫子班傑明‧哈里森，他】

A noun in apposition may come between antecedent and relative, because in such a combination no real ambiguity can arise.

作為同位語的名詞可以放在先行詞和關係從句之間，因為在這類組合中並不會產生真正的歧義。

例如：

the Duke of York, his brother, who was regarded with hostility by the Whigs 【約克公爵，他的兄弟，被輝格黨視為敵對的】

補充說明 3：修飾語（定、狀語）和中心詞放在一起。

Modifiers should come, if possible, next to the words they modify. If several expressions modify the same word, they should be arranged so that no wrong relation is suggested.

修飾語應該盡可能靠近它們所修飾的詞。如果同一個詞有好幾組修飾語，這些修飾語應該正確排列，以避免表達出錯誤的修飾關係。

例如：

All the members were not present.【所有成員都不在場。】

Not all the members were present.【並非所有成員都在場。】

Part 1　運用與組合規則

She only found two mistakes.【她只發現了兩個錯誤。】

The director said he hoped all members would give generously to the Fund at a meeting of the committee yesterday.【主任表示，他曾希望所有成員在昨天的委員會會議上都慷慨地向基金捐款。】

Major R. E. Joyce will give a lecture on Tuesday evening in Bailey Hall, to which the public is invited on "My Experiences in Mesopotamia" at 8:00 P. M.【R·E· 喬伊斯少校將於週二晚上在貝利大廳發表演講，公眾將在晚上 8 點受邀參加「我在美索不達米亞的經歷」。】

She found only two mistakes.【她發現只有兩個錯誤。】

At a meeting of the committee yesterday, the director said he hoped all members would give generously to the Fund.【在昨天的委員會會議上，主任說他希望所有成員都慷慨地向基金捐款。】

On Tuesday evening at eight, Major R. E. Joyce will give a lecture in Bailey Hall on "My Experiences in Mesopotamia". The public is invited.【週二晚上 8 點，R·E· 喬伊斯少校將在貝利大廳就「我在美索不達米亞的經歷」發表演講。公眾將被邀請。】

Note, in the last left-hand example, how swiftly meaning departs when words are wrongly juxtaposed.

注意，在最後一組例句的左邊版本中，詞序錯誤安排時，含義如何立刻改變。

2-10　摘要的寫作

Rule 21　In summaries, keep to one tense
規則二十一　在摘要中，只用一種時態

【問題 1】摘要的時態

In summarizing the action of a drama, use the present tense. In summarizing a poem, story, or novel, also use the present, though you may use the past if it seems more natural to do so. If the summary is in the present tense, antecedent action should be expressed by the perfect; if in the past, by the past perfect.

概述一個劇本的情節用現在式。概述一首詩歌、一個故事、一部小說，也用現在式，當然，使用過去時會顯得更自然的話，也可以使用過去式。如果概述部分用現在式，那麼

之前發生的事應該用現在完成式來表達；如果概述部分用過去式，之前發生的事用過去完成式。

例如：

Chance prevents Friar John from delivering Friar Lawrence's letter to Romeo. Meanwhile, owing to her father's arbitrary change of the day set for her wedding, Juliet has been compelled to drink the potion on Tuesday night, with the result that Balthasar informs Romeo of her supposed death before Friar Lawrence learns of the nondelivery of the letter. 【突發事件阻礙了約翰神父把勞倫斯神父的信送給羅密歐。同時，由於茱麗葉的父親蠻橫地改變了女兒的婚期，茱麗葉不得不在週二晚上喝下了麻藥，結果，在勞倫斯神父得知信件尚未送達之前，鮑爾薩澤就已經把茱麗葉死亡的傳聞告知了羅密歐。】

Shifting from one tense to another gives the appearance of uncertainty and irresolution.

在時態之間來回切換會給人一種不確定、不果斷的印象。

注意：需要使用不同時態的唯一例外情況。

But whichever tense is used in the summary, a past tense in indirect discourse or in indirect question remains unchanged. Apart from the exceptions noted, the writer should use the same tense throughout.

但是無論概述中使用哪種時態,間接引語或間接問句中原本的過去時態都保持不變。除這個例外情況,作者應該使用統一時態貫穿全文。

例如:

The Friar confesses that it was he who married them. 【神父承認之前是他為他們證婚的。】

【問題 2】概要的提示

In presenting the statements or the thought of someone else, as in summarizing an essay or reporting a speech, do not overwork such expressions as "he said", "she stated", "the speaker added", "the speaker then went on to say", "the author also thinks". Indicate clearly at the outset, once for all, that what follows is summary, and then waste no words in repeating the notification.

在轉述他人的言論或思想時,比如概述一篇短文或一段演講時,不要過多使用諸如「he said」、「she stated」、「the speaker added」、「the speaker then went on to say」、「the author also thinks」等表達。在開頭一次性說明,接下來寫的內容都是概述,之後就不用浪費筆墨反覆說明了。

Part 1　運用與組合規則

【問題 3】概要的作用

In notebooks, in newspapers, in handbooks of literature, summaries of one kind or another may be indispensable, and for children in primary schools retelling a story in their own words is a useful exercise.

在筆記、報紙和文學手記中，各種摘要是必不可少的，對於小學生來說，用自己的話複述一個故事是有用的練習。

【問題 4】文學評論不是概要

But in the criticism or interpretation of literature, be careful to avoid dropping into summary. It may be necessary to devote one or two sentences to indicating the subject, or the opening situation, of the work being discussed, or to cite numerous details to illustrate its qualities. But you should aim at writing an orderly discussion supported by evidence, not a summary with occasional comment.

Similarly, if the scope of the discussion includes a number of works, as a rule it is better not to take them up singly in chronological order but to aim from the beginning at establishing general conclusions.

但是文學評論或解說，則要注意，不要淪為摘要。用一兩個句子說明所要討論的作品的主題、背景，或者引用大量細節來說明該作品的特點,也許是必要的。但是你應該旨在寫出一篇有論據支撐的、有條理的論文,而不是夾雜著少量評論的摘要。

同樣地,如果論述的範圍涉及若干作品,則最好不要按照年代順序逐個排列出來,而是要一開始就要確立一個總論點。

2-11 句子結尾表強調

Rule 22　Place the emphatic words of a sentence at the end

規則二十二　要把一個句子中強調的詞(組)放在句末

The proper place in the sentence for the word or group of words that the writer desires to make most prominent is usually the end.

一個句子中作者想要強調的詞或片語,最恰當的位置通常在句末。

例如：

Humanity has hardly advanced in fortitude since that time, though it has advanced in many other ways. (✗)【自那時以來，人類的力量幾乎沒有進步，儘管它在許多其他方面取得了進步。】

Since that time, humanity has advanced in many ways, but it has hardly advanced in fortitude. (✓)【從那時起，人類在許多方面都取得了進步，但它的力量幾乎沒有進步。】

This steel is principally used for making razors, because of its hardness. (✗)【這種鋼主要用於製造剃鬚刀，因為它的硬度。】

Because of its hardness, this steel is used principally for making razors. (✓)【由於它的硬度，這種鋼主要用於製造刮鬍刀。】

The word or group of words entitled to this position of prominence is usually the logical predicate—that is, the new element in the sentence, as it is in the second example.

被放在這個突出位置的詞或片語，通常是邏輯謂語——也就是，一個句子中新的資訊要素，就像例句二那樣。

The effectiveness of the periodic sentence arises from the prominence it gives to the main statement.

2-11　句子結尾表強調

　　掉尾句（圓周句）之所以是更有效果的表達，就是因為它突出了主要資訊陳述。

例如：

Four centuries ago, Christopher Columbus, one of the Italian mariners whom the decline of their own republics had put at the service of the world and of adventure, seeking for Spain a westward passage to the Indies to offset the achievement of Portuguese discoverers, lighted on America. With these hopes and in this belief I would urge you, laying aside all hindrance, thrusting away all private aims, to devote yourself unswervingly and unflinchingly to the vigorous and successful prosecution of this war.

【四個世紀前，許多義大利航海家，由於本國的衰落，而不得不放眼世界去探險，克里斯多福‧哥倫布（Christopher Columbus）就是其中一員。他在為西班牙尋求向西通往印度群島的航線，以匹敵葡萄牙探險家的成就時，發現了美洲大陸。懷著同樣的希望與信念，我熱切期望您放下一切阻礙，摒棄一切私欲，堅定不移地、義無反顧地投入這場勢頭正勁的戰爭。】

The other prominent position in the sentence is the beginning. Any element in the sentence other than the subject becomes emphatic when placed first.

句子中另一個可以有強調突出效果的是句首。一個句子中除了主語以外的任何成分放在句首時，都成為被強調的部分。

例如：

Deceit or treachery she could never forgive.【欺騙或背叛，是她永遠無法原諒的。】

Vast and rude, fretted by the action of nearly three thousand years, the fragments of this architecture may often seem, at first sight, like works of nature.【龐大而粗糙，經過近三千年的侵蝕，這座建築的殘垣斷壁，乍看起來，就好像是自然天成的。】

Home is the sailor.【家，水手回來了。】

A subject coming first in its sentence may be emphatic, but hardly by its position alone.

放在句首的主語也許是被強調的，但並不只是由於它所在的位置。

例如：

"Great kings worshiped at his shrine."【「偉大的國王在他的神殿供奉。」】

In the sentence, the emphasis upon kings arises largely from its meaning and from the context.

2-11 句子結尾表強調

在上述句子中，對於 kings 的強調相當程度上來自於這個詞的含義和上下文語境。

To receive special emphasis, the subject of a sentence must take the position of the predicate.

如果要特別強調一個句子的主語，那就必須將這個句子的主謂語倒裝。

例如：

Through the middle of the valley flowed a winding stream. 【一條蜿蜒的溪流穿過山谷的中央。】

The principle that the proper place for what is to be made most prominent is the end applies equally to the words of a sentence, to the sentences of a paragraph, and to the paragraphs of a composition.

最能產生突出強調作用的位置是末尾。這條原則不僅適用於一個句子中所有的詞，一個段落中所有的句子，也適用於一篇文章中所有的段落。

Part 1　運用與組合規則

Part 2　格式與用詞規範

3-1　Colloquialisms 口語

If you use a colloquialism or a slang word or phrase, simply use it; do not draw attention to it by enclosing it in quotation marks. To do so is to put on airs, as though you were inviting the reader to join you in a select society of those who know better.

如果你要使用成語或俚語，直接寫出來就可以；不要把它們放在引號中引起注意。這麼做就是裝腔作勢，就好像你在邀請讀者和你一起加入菁英社會似的。

3-2　Exclamations 感嘆句

Do not attempt to emphasize simple statements by using a mark of exclamation.

不要試圖用驚嘆號來強調一個簡單的陳述句。

例如：

It was a wonderful show!（✗）【這是一場精采的秀！】

It was a wonderful show.（✓）【這是一場精采的秀。】

The exclamation mark is to be reserved for use after true exclamations or commands.

驚嘆號只能用在真正的感嘆句或命令句之後。

例如：

What a wonderful show!（√）【多麼精采的一場秀呀！】

Halt!（√）【停住！】

3-3　Headings 標題

　　If a manuscript is to be submitted for publication, leave plenty of space at the top of page 1. The editor will need this space to write directions to the compositor. Place the heading, or title, at least a fourth of the way down the page. Leave a blank line, or its equivalent in space, after the heading. On succeeding pages, begin near the top, but not so near as to give a crowded appearance. Omit the period after a title or heading. A question mark or an exclamation point may be used if the heading calls for it.

　　如果一部手稿要交付出版，則要在第一頁上方留出較大的空白。編輯需要利用這個空白處給排版工人寫指示。這一頁要至少留出占整個頁面1/4面積的空白，然後再接著書寫標題或書名。標題下面要空一行，或相當於一行的間距。之後的每一頁，都要從接近頁面頂部的位置開始書寫，但是不

Part 2　格式與用詞規範

要太靠近邊緣,而給人擁擠的印象。刪除標題或書名之後的句號。如有必要,標題之後可以使用問號或驚嘆號。

3-4　Hyphen 連字符號

When two or more words are combined to form a compound adjective, a hyphen is usually required.

兩個及以上單片語合成複合形容詞時,通常要使用連字符號。

例如：

He belonged to the leisure class and enjoyed leisure-class pursuits.【他屬於有閒階級,有著有閒階級的追求。】

She entered her boat in the round-the-island race.【她讓她的小艇參加了環島航行比賽。】

Do not use a hyphen between words that can better be written as one word:

如果合成詞能融合成一個無需連字符號的單字會更好:

例如：

water-fowl ➡ waterfowl 【水鳥】

3-4　Hyphen 連字符號

Common sense will aid you in the decision, but a dictionary is more reliable. The steady evolution of the language seems to favor union: two words eventually become one, usually after a period of hyphenation.

常識有助於判斷，但字典更可靠。語言的逐漸演變似乎是趨向於融合成一個詞：一般地，最開始分開寫的兩個詞，然後透過連字符號連線，使用一段時間後，最終合為一詞。

例如：

bed chamber ➡ bed-chamber ➡ bedchamber 【臥室】

wild life ➡ wild-life ➡ wildlife 【野生動植物】

bell boy ➡ bell-boy ➡ bellboy 【門僮】

The hyphen can play tricks on the unwary, as it did in Chattanooga when two newspapers merged — the News and the Free Press. Someone introduced a hyphen into the merger, and the paper became The Chattanooga News-Free Press, which sounds as though the paper were news-free, or devoid of news. Obviously, we ask too much of a hyphen when we ask it to cast its spell over words it does not adjoin.

連字符號會作弄那些粗心大意的人，就像在 Chattanooga 的兩家報紙 —— the News 與 the Free Press 合併的情形那樣。有人在合併名稱中使用了一個連字符號，合併後報紙名稱寫作 The Chattanooga News-Free Press，news-free 一詞使該報紙聽上去就好像是沒有新聞或缺少新聞一樣。顯然，如果在連字符號不能連線的詞之間，我們也使用連字符號，就對它要求過多了。

3-5　Margins 頁邊距

Keep right-hand and left-hand margins roughly the same width.

在頁面的左右兩側都留下大約等寬的空白。

Exception: If a great deal of annotating or editing is anticipated, the left-hand margin should be roomy enough to accommodate this work.

例外情況：如果預見到要做的旁注或修改比較多，則左側的留白要足夠大，以適應這些工作需求。

3-6　Numerals 數字

Do not spell out dates or other serial numbers. Write them in figures or in Roman notation, as appropriate.

不要把日期或序列數字拼寫成單字。用阿拉伯數字或羅馬數字書寫才恰當。

例如：

August 9, 1988　【1988 年 8 月 9 日】

Part XII　【第十二章】

Rule 3　【規則三】

352d Infantry　【第 352 步兵團】

Exception: When they occur in dialogue, most dates and numbers are best spelled out.

例外情況：當出現在對話中時，大部分日期和數字還是要拼寫成單字。

例如：

I arrived home on August ninth.　【我是 8 月 9 號到家的。】

In the year 2004, I turned twenty-one.　【2004 年，我 21 歲。】

Read Chapter Twelve.　【讀第十二章。】

3-7　Parentheses 圓括號

A sentence containing an expression in parentheses is punctuated outside the last mark of parenthesis exactly as if the parenthetical expression were absent. The expression within the marks is punctuated as if it stood by itself, except that the final stop is omitted unless it is a question mark or an exclamation point.

一個句子中包含的用括號括起來的語言片段，並不影響括號之外的標點使用。可以說這個括號內的片段是游離於句子之外的部分。括在括號內的語言片段，如果中間需要使用標點，把這個語言片段看作是獨立的，根據其自身情況而定，但括號內語言片段的末尾不能有標點，除非是問號或驚嘆號。

例如：

I went to her house yesterday (my third attempt to see her), but she had left town. 【我昨天去了她家（這是我第三次去看她了），但她已經出城了。】

He declares (and why should we doubt his good faith?) that he is now certain of success. 【他宣稱（而我們為什麼要懷疑他的堅定信念呢？）他現在確定會成功。】

(When a wholly detached expression or sentence is parenthesized, the final stop comes before the last mark of parenthesis.)

（當括號內的語言片段是獨立完整的句子時，句子末尾的標點也要放在括號內。）

3-8　Quotations 引文

Formal quotations cited as documentary evidence are introduced by a colon and enclosed in quotation marks.

作為文獻依據的正式引文要用冒號引出，並放在雙引號之中。

例如：

The United States Coast Pilot has this to say of the place: "Bracy Cove, 0.5 mile eastward of Bear Island, is exposed to southeast winds, has a rocky and uneven bottom, and is unfit for anchorage."【美國沿海領港員談及該地時說：「位於熊島以東半英里處的布萊西灣常受東南風的侵襲，而且海底岩石林立，凹凸不平，因此不宜拋錨。」】

A quotation grammatically in apposition or the direct object of a verb is preceded by a comma and enclosed in quotation marks.

文法上作為同位語或動詞直接賓語的引文，其前要加上逗號，並且整段引文應置於雙引號內。

例如：

I am reminded of the advice of my neighbor, "Never worry about your heart till it stops beating." 【我常想起我鄰居的忠告，「心臟停止跳動之前都不要為之擔憂。」】

Mark Twain says, "A classic is something that everybody wants to have read and nobody wants to read." 【馬克·吐溫說：「名著就是人人都希望讀過但從沒有人想讀的書。」】

When a quotation is followed by an attributive phrase, the comma is enclosed within the quotation marks.

當引文之後接一個修飾片語時，引文末尾的逗號要放在雙引號內。

例如："I can't attend," she said. 【「我不能參加，」她說。】

Typographical usage dictates that the comma be inside the marks, though logically it often seems not to belong there.

按照印刷慣例，逗號要放在雙引號內，儘管從邏輯上看這經常是不合理的。

3-8　Quotations 引文

例如：

"The Fish", "Poetry", and "The Monkeys" are in *Marianne Moore's Selected Poems*. 【「魚」、「詩」和「猴子」都在《瑪麗安・穆爾詩歌選集》中。】

When quotations of an entire line, or more, of either verse or prose are to be distinguished typographically from text matter, as are the quotations in this book, begin on a fresh line and indent. Quotation marks should not be used unless they appear in the original, as in dialogue.

當詩歌或散文中的整行或更多的內容作為引文，需要從印刷上區別於文中其他內容時，（就像本書中的引文那樣），這段引文要另起一行，並縮排。這樣的引文通常不應該使用雙引號，除非原文中出現象對話中那樣的引號。

例如：

Wordsworth's enthusiasm for the French Revolution was at first unbounded: Bliss was it in that dawn to be alive, but to be young was very heaven! 【華茲華斯對於法國大革命的熱情最初是無限的：在那個黎明，活著是幸福的，但年輕是天堂！】

Quotations introduced by that are indirect discourse and not enclosed in quotation marks.

由 that 引導的間接引語不要用雙引號。

例如：

Keats declares that beauty is truth, truth beauty.【濟慈宣稱美就是真理，真理之美。】

Dickinson states that a coffin is a small domain.【狄金生說棺材是一個小領域。】

Proverbial expressions and familiar phrases of literary origin require no quotation marks.

諺語或來自文學作品但廣為人知的熟語不需要用雙引號。

例如：

These are the times that try men's souls.【這是考驗人類靈魂的時代。】

He lives far from the madding crowd.【他遠離瘋狂的人群很遠居住。】

3-9　References 參考數據

In scholarly work requiring exact references, abbreviate titles that occur frequently, giving the full forms in an alphabetical list at the end. As a general practice, give the references in parentheses or in footnotes, not in the body of the sentence. Omit the words act, scene, line, book, volume, page, except when referring to only one of them.

在要求標明確切參考資料的學術作品中，先縮略書寫頻繁出現的標題，然後再在作品結尾部分按照字母順序列出這些縮略標題的全稱。依據慣例，把參考資料寫在括號內或腳註內，而不要寫在句子正文中。省略 act（幕）、scene（場）、line（行）、book（冊）、volume（卷）、page（頁）等詞，除非只用到其中一個。

Punctuate as indicated below: in the second scene of the third act in III. ii Better still, simply insert III. ii in parentheses at the proper place in the sentence.

具體標點斷句方式如下：更好的處理方式是直接把（III. ii）第三幕第二場，放到括號裡，插入到句子中合適位置。

例如：

After the killing of Polonius, Hamlet is placed under guard (*IV. ii. 14*). 【波隆尼爾被殺後，哈姆雷特被置於看守之下（第四幕，第二場，第 14 頁）。】

2 Samuel i: 17 —— 27 【撒母耳記，下卷，第一章，第 17 頁至第 27 頁】

Othello II. iii. 264 —— 267; III. iii. 155 —— 161【《奧賽羅》，第二幕，第三場，第 264 頁至第 267 頁；第三幕，第三場，第 155 頁至第 161 頁】

3-10　Syllabication 音節劃分

When a word must be divided at the end of a line, consult a dictionary to learn the syllables between which division should be made. The student will do well to examine the syllable division in a number of pages of any carefully printed book.

當一個單字寫到一行的末尾處，須切斷移行時，要查閱字典了解這個單字的音節劃分，以便確定單字可以切斷的恰當位置。學生仔細研究幾頁印刷考究的書籍中的音節劃分，就能夠做好。

3-11　Titles 書名

For the titles of literary works, scholarly usage prefers italics with capitalized initials. The usage of editors and publishers varies, some using italics with capitalized initials, others using Roman with capitalized initials and with or without quotation marks. Use italics (indicated in manuscript by underscoring) except in writing for a periodical that follows a different practice. Omit initial A or The from titles when you place the possessive before them.

文學作品的標題，學術上的慣例傾向於用斜體字配合首字母大寫。而編輯和出版商的用法則各有不同，有人用斜體字加首字母大寫，有人用正體字加首字母大寫，有人用引號有人不用。除非是為遵循特殊慣例的期刊寫文章，否則一般還是用斜體字（如果是手稿可以用下劃線表示）。書名前如果使用所有格時，要把書名開頭的冠詞去掉。

例如：

A Tale of Two Cities; Dickens's *Tale of Two Cities*. 【《雙城記》；狄更斯的《雙城記》。】

The Age of Innocence; Wharton's *Age of Innocence*. 【《純真年代》；華頓的《純真年代》。】

4-1　常錯詞 1-10

1. Aggravate / Irritate.

The first means "to add to" an already troublesome or vexing matter or condition. The second means "to vex" or "to annoy" or "to chafe".

aggravate 意思是讓一個已經令人煩惱的事情或狀況變得更嚴重。irritate 意思是使（開始）煩惱、生氣或急躁。

2. All right.

Idiomatic in familiar speech as a detached phrase in the sense "Agreed", or "Go ahead," or "O. K.". Properly written as two words — all right.

在熟人之間交談時，獨立使用的一個慣用語。意思相當於「同意」、「繼續吧」、「好的」。正確的寫法是分成兩個詞 all 和 right。

3. Allude.

Do not confuse with elude. You allude to a book; you elude a pursuer. Note, too, that allude is not synonymous with refer. An allusion is an indirect mention, a reference is a specific one.

不要和 elude 混淆。你可以用 allude 表達「提到一本書」；而用 elude 表達「躲避一個追求者」。還要注意：allude 也不是 refer 的同義詞。allusion 是指間接的提及，而 reference 是詳細地說起。

4. Allusion.

Easily confused with illusion. The first means "an indirect reference"; the second means "an unreal image" or "a false impression".

這個詞容易與 illusion 混淆。allusion 的意思是間接提及；而 illusion 則是指「不真實的影像」或「錯誤的印象」。

5. Alternate / Alternative.

The words are not always interchangeable as nouns or adjectives. The first means every other one in a series; the second, one of two possibilities. As the other one of a series of two, an alternate may stand for "a substitute", but an alternative, although used in a similar sense, connotes a matter of choice that is never present with alternate.

這兩個詞可作為名詞或形容詞，但含義不盡相同。alternate 指在一個序列中每間隔一個交替出現；而 alternative 則是指兩種可能性中的一種。作為同系列兩個選項中的另一個，alternate 可以代表替代物本身；儘管 alternative 也有類似的含義，但與 alternate 相比多了一層「選擇」的意味。

例如：

As the flooded road left them no alternative, they took the alternate route. 【由於道路被淹，他們別無選擇，只好走了另一條路線。】

6. Among / Between.

When more than two things or persons are involved, among is usually called for:

當涉及兩個以上的人或事物時，介詞通常要用 among：

例如：

The money was divided among the four players. 【這筆錢被分配給了四名球員。】

When, however, more than two are involved but each is considered individually, between is preferred:

然而，當涉及兩個以上的人或事物，但要強調其中每個單獨個體時，用 between 更好：

例如：

an agreement between the six heirs 【六位繼承人之間的協議】

7. And / Or.

A device, or shortcut, that damages a sentence and often leads to confusion or ambiguity.

and、or 雖是簡短的連線，卻經常打斷一個句子，造成混亂和歧義。

例如：

First of all, would an honor system successfully cut down on the amount of stealing and / or cheating?（×）【首先，(監獄的)榮譽系統能否成功減少偷竊和／或作弊事件？】

First of all, would an honor system reduce the incidence of stealing or cheating or both?（√）【首先，(監獄的)榮譽系統會減少偷竊還是作弊事件，還是都可以？】

8. Anticipate.

Use expect in the sense of simple expectation.

僅表示「預料」含義時，用 expect 就可以了。

例如：

I anticipated that he would look older.（×）【我預計他會看起來更老。】

I expected that he would look older.（√）【我本以為他看起來會更老。】

My brother anticipated the upturn in the market. (✗)
【我哥哥已料到市場的好轉。】

My brother expected the upturn in the market. (√)
【我哥哥預計市場會好轉。】

In the second example, the word anticipated is ambiguous. It could mean simply that the brother believed the upturn would occur, or it could mean that he acted in advance of the expected upturn — by buying stock, perhaps.

在第二組例句中，anticipated 這個詞有歧義。它的意思可以是哥哥相信上漲行情會發生，也可以是他在預料到行情上漲時提前採取了行動 —— 比如買入股票。

9. Anybody.

In the sense of "any person", not to be written as two words. Anybody means "any corpse", or "any human form", or "any group". The rule holds equally for everybody, nobody, and somebody.

表示「任何人」的含義時，不要寫成分開的兩個詞。any ＋ body 的意思是「任何一具屍體」、「任何人形」或「任何體系」。這種情況同樣適用於含有 body 的不定代詞 everybody、nobody 和 somebody。

10. Anyone.

In the sense of "anybody", written as one word. Any one means "any single person" or "any single thing".

表示「任何人」時,合在一起寫成一個詞。分開寫成 any one,意思可以是「任何一個單獨的人」或「任何一個單獨的事物」。

4-2　常錯詞 11-20

11. As good or better than.

Expressions of this type should be corrected by rearranging the sentences.

這種類型的表達應該透過重新排列句子內部的詞語來改正。

例如:

My opinion is as good or better than his.（✗）【我的意見和他的一樣好或更好。】

My opinion is as good as his, or better (if not better) .（✓）【我的意見和他的一樣好,或者更好(如果不是更好的話)。】

Part 2　格式與用詞規範

12. As to whether.

Whether is sufficient.

單獨使用 whether 就足夠了。

13. As yet.

Yet nearly always is as good, if not better.

單獨使用一個 yet 就可以了，表達效果不會更差。

例如：

No agreement has been reached as yet.【目前尚未達成協議。】

No agreement has yet been reached.【尚未達成協議。】

The chief exception is at the beginning of a sentence, where yet means something different.

用於句首的時候，兩者含義不同。as yet 仍然表示「還沒……」，而單獨的 yet 表示轉折。

例如：

Yet (or despite everything) he has not succeeded.【然而（或儘管如此）他並沒有成功。】

As yet (or so far) he has not succeeded.【到目前為止（或迄今為止）他還沒有成功。】

14. Being.

Not appropriate after regard...as.

being 不能用於片語 regard...as「認為」之後。

例如：

He is regarded as being the best dancer in the club. (✗)【他被認為是俱樂部裡最好的舞者。】

He is regarded as the best dancer in the club. (√)【他被認為是俱樂部裡最好的舞者。】

15. But.

Unnecessary after doubt and help.

在 no doubt 無疑、not help 不得不之後，不必用 but。

例如：

I have no doubt but that (✗)【我毫不懷疑，但】

I have no doubt that (√)【我毫不懷疑】

he could not help but see that (✗)【他不禁而是看到】

he could not help seeing that (√)【他不禁看到】

The too-frequent use of but as a conjunction leads to the fault discussed under Rule 18. A loose sentence formed with but can usually be converted into a periodic sentence formed with although.

過於頻繁地使用 but 作為連線詞,會引發規則十八(也就是使用一連串鬆散句)的問題。頻繁使用 but 造成的鬆散句,通常可以透過轉換為 although 改為掉尾句。

Particularly awkward is one but closely following another, thus making a contrast to a contrast, or a reservation to a reservation. This is easily corrected by rearrangement.

尤其彆扭的情況是一個 but 緊接另一個 but,造成對比中又有對比,或讓步中又有讓步的複雜結構。這種情況透過重組句子結構容易修改。

例如:

Our country had vast resources but seemed almost wholly unprepared for war. But within a year it had created an army of four million. (✗)【我們的國家擁有豐富的資源,但似乎完全沒有	Our country seemed almost wholly unprepared for war, but it had vast resources. Within a year it had created an army of four million. (√)【我們的國家似乎完全沒有為戰爭做好準備,但它擁有

為戰爭做好準備。但在一年之內，它就組建了一支四百萬人的軍隊。】 豐富的資源，一年之內，就組建了一支四百萬人的軍隊。】

16. Can.

Means "am (is, are) able". Not to be used as a substitute for may.

意思是「有能力做⋯⋯」。不能代替 may（允許）。

17. Care less.

The dismissive "I couldn't care less" is often used with the shortened "not" mistakenly (and mysteriously) omitted: "I could care less." The error destroys the meaning of the sentence and is careless indeed.

用 I couldn't care less（我不可能更不在乎了）來表達輕視、蔑視地以為，經常會誤將其中縮寫的否定詞 not 遺漏掉，寫成 I could care less（我可以更不在乎）。這種錯誤完全是馬虎造成的，會讓整個句子意思完全相反。

18. Case.

Often unnecessary.

case（情況、案例）這個詞常常是沒有必要使用的。

例如：

In many cases, the rooms lacked air conditioning. (✗)【在許多情況下，房間沒有冷氣。】

Many of the rooms lacked air conditioning. (✓)【許多房間沒有冷氣。】

It has rarely been the case that any mistake has been made. (✗)【犯錯誤的情況很少見。】

Few mistakes have been made. (✓)【幾乎沒有犯過錯誤。】

19. Certainly.

Used indiscriminately by some speakers, much as others use very, in an attempt to intensify any and every statement. A mannerism of this kind, bad in speech, is even worse in writing.

許多人在口語中任意地使用 certainly 這個詞，就像 very 一樣頻繁，目的是強調每一句話。這種習慣在口語中不好，在寫作中則更糟。

20. Character.

Often simply redundant, used from a mere habit of wordiness.

性質，這個詞常常純粹就是多餘的，僅僅就是一種囉唆的習慣。

4-3　常錯詞 21-30

21. Claim (verb).

With object-noun, means "lay claim to." May be used with a dependent clause if this sense is clearly intended:

其後接一個作賓語的名詞時，意為「主張、申稱」。而且如果明確表達上述含義時，其後也可以接一個獨立從句：

例如：

She claimed that she was the sole heir.【她聲稱她是唯一繼承人。】

But even here claimed to be would be better.

但是在此處，在 claim 之後銜接 to be 要更好一些。也就是 She claimed to be the sole heir.

Not to be used as a substitute for declare, maintain, or charge.

claim 不可以替代 declare（宣布，宣告）、maintain（堅持認為）或 charge（指責）來使用。

例如：

He claimed he knew how.

【他聲稱自己知道怎麼做。（有偏主觀的意味，客觀上是不確定的）】

He declared he knew how.

【他宣告自己知道怎麼做。（帶有明確、肯定的意味）】

22. Clever.

Note that the word means one thing when applied to people, another when applied to horses. A clever horse is a good-natured one, not an ingenious one.

clever 用來修飾馬的時候，和修飾人的時候，含義不同。修飾人時意思是「聰明的」，而修飾馬時意思是「溫馴的」。

23. Compare.

To compare to is to point out or imply resemblances between objects regarded as essentially of a different order; to compare with is mainly to point out differences between objects regarded as essentially of the same order. Thus, life has been compared to a pilgrimage, to a drama, to a battle; Congress may be compared with the British Parliament.

Paris has been compared to ancient Athens; it may be compared with modern London.

片語「to compare to」是指出本質上屬於不同類別的兩個事物之間的相似之處；片語「to compare with」是指出本質上屬於相同類別的兩個事物之間的不同之處。因此，「人生」可以 compare to「一次朝聖之旅」、「一齣戲」、「一場戰鬥」；「國會」可以 compare with「英國議會」。

「巴黎」與古希臘的雅典相比用 compare to，與現代倫敦相比則用 compare with。

24. Comprise.

Literally, "embrace": A zoo comprises mammals, reptiles, and birds (because it "embraces", or "includes", them). But animals do not comprise ("embrace") a zoo — they constitute a zoo.

字面意思等於「embrace」（包含），如：一個動物園 comprise（包含）哺乳動物、爬行動物和鳥類。或者說哺乳動物、爬行動物和鳥類是動物園的成員［因為動物園「embrace」（包含）或「include」（包括）這些動物］。但上一句話的主賓語對調位置，就不成立了。動物們不能 comprise 或 embrace（包含）一個動物園，它們只能 constitute（組成）一個動物園。

Part 2　格式與用詞規範

25. Consider.

Not followed by as when it means "believe to be".

當表示「認為（……怎麼樣）」的意思時，其後不接介詞 as。

例如：

I consider him as competent.（✗）【我認為他有能力。】

I consider him competent.（✓）【我認為他有能力。】

When considered means "examined" or "discussed", it is followed by as:

而表示「考慮」或「說成」（……是什麼）的含義時，其後要接介詞 as：

例如：

The lecturer considered Eisenhower first as soldier and second as administrator.【演講者說艾森豪首先是士兵，其次才是管理者。】

26. Contact.

As a transitive verb, the word is vague and self-important. Do not contact people; get in touch with them, look them up, phone them, find them, or meet them.

作為及物動詞使用時，contact 含義比較模糊，而且有一種妄自尊大的意味。所以不要以人作為 contact 的賓語；要表示「聯絡」這類含義時，可以用 get in touch 表示接觸某人、用 look up 表示看望某人、用 phone 表示打電話給某人，用 find 表示找人，meet 表示與人會面。

27. Cope.

An intransitive verb used with "with". In formal writing, one doesn't "cope", one "copes with" something or somebody.

cope 是一個不及物動詞，其後要接介詞 with 才能帶賓語。在正式寫作中，要表達「處理」某事物、「應對」某人的含義時，不要只用 cope，而要用 cope with。

例如：

I knew they'd cope. (jocular) 【我知道他們會應付的。（非正式場合）】

I knew they would cope with the situation. 【我知道他們會應付這種情況。】

28. Currently.

In the sense of now with a verb in the present tense, currently is usually redundant; emphasis is better achieved through a more precise reference to time.

當謂語動詞是現在時態，再在句子中用一個 currently 表示「現在」的含義，往往顯得多餘；如果要強調時間，那麼使用更精確、更具體的時間片語會更好，如 at this moment「此刻」。

例如：

We are currently reviewing your application.（✗）【我們目前正在稽核您的申請。】

We are at this moment reviewing your application.（√）【我們目前正在稽核您的申請。】

29. Data.

Like strata, phenomena, and media, data is a plural and is best used with a plural verb. The word, however, is slowly gaining acceptance as a singular.

data 數據這個詞表達的是一種複數的概念，要配合複數的謂語動詞使用，類似的詞還有：strata（階級）、phenomena（現象）和 media（媒體）等。當然，數據這個詞也正在作為一個單數概念逐漸被人們所接受。

例如：

The data is misleading.【數據具有誤導性。】

These data are misleading.【這些數據具有誤導性。】

30. Different than.

Here logic supports established usage: one thing differs from another, hence, different from. Or, other than, unlike.

這是一個不合乎習慣的組合方式。當要表達「不同於」這種邏輯關係時,最好還是用慣用語:differ from 或 different from 不同於, other than 而不是, unlike 不像……等。

4-4 常錯詞 31-40

31. Disinterested.

Means "impartial". Do not confuse it with uninterested, which means "not interested in".

這個詞的意思是「公正無私的,不偏袒的」。不要把它跟表示「不感興趣」的 uninterested 一詞混淆。

例如:

Let a disinterested person judge our dispute. (an impartial person) 【讓一個無私的人來判斷我們的爭論。(一個不偏不倚的人)】

This man is obviously uninterested in our dispute. (couldn't care less) 【這個人顯然對我們的爭論不感興趣。(不在乎)】

32. Divided into.

Not to be misused for composed of. The line is sometimes difficult to draw; doubtless plays are divided into acts, but poems are composed of stanzas. An apple, halved, is divided into sections, but an apple is composed of seeds, flesh, and skin.

不要把這個片語等同於 composed of 而誤用。雖然這兩個片語之間的差異有時很難劃分清楚，都有「分」的含義。但無疑的是，戲劇分成幾幕的「分」要用 divide into，而詩歌分成幾節的「分」則要用 compose of。把一個蘋果切分成兩半的「分」要用 divide into，而一個蘋果組成要件可以分為種子、果肉和果皮的「分」則要用 compose of。

33. Due to.

Loosely used for through, because of, or owing to, in adverbial phrases.

due to 作為狀語片語時，常常被隨意地用於表達 through（透過）、because of（因為）、owing to（由於）等介詞或介詞片語表達的邏輯關係。（以下例句中 due to 的使用是不恰當的。）

例如：

He lost the first game due to carelessness.（✗）【由於粗心，他輸掉了第一場比賽。】

He lost the first game because of carelessness.（√）【由於粗心，他輸掉了第一場比賽。】

In correct use, synonymous with attributable to:

due to 的正確用法是與片語 attributable to 同義，表示「歸因於……」

例如：

The accident was due to bad weather.【事故歸因於惡劣天氣。】

losses due to preventable fires 【損失歸因於本可預防的火災】

34. Each and every one.

Pitchman's jargon. Avoid, except in dialogue.

這個片語是小商販的俚語。除了日常對話外，盡量還是別用。

例如：

It should be a lesson to each and every one of us.（✗）【這應該給我們每個人一個教訓。】

It should be a lesson to every one of us (to us all).（√）【這應該給我們每個人一個教訓。】

35. Effect.

As a noun, means "result"; as a verb, means "to bring about", "to accomplish" (not to be confused with affect, which means "to influence").

作為名詞，意思是「效果」；作為動詞，意思是「帶來」或「實現」(不要與 affect 混淆，affect 的意思是「影響」)。

As a noun, often loosely used in perfunctory writing about fashions, music, painting, and other arts:

effect 作為一個名詞，經常被隨意地用於有關流行、音樂、繪畫及其他藝術類文章中：

例如：

a Southwestern effect 【西南效應】

effects in pale green 【淡綠色的效果】

very delicate effects 【非常柔和的感覺】

subtle effects 【微妙的影響】

a charming effect was produced 【產生了迷人的效果】

The writer who has a definite meaning to express will not take refuge in such vagueness.

但明確知道自己要表達什麼的作者，是不會這麼含糊其辭的。

36. Enormity.

Use only in the sense of "monstrous wickedness". Misleading, if not wrong, when used to express bigness.

這個詞只能用來表達「罪大惡極」的含義。如果用於表達「巨大」的含義，即使不算錯，也有一定的誤導性。

37. Enthuse.

An annoying verb growing out of the noun enthusiasm. Not recommended.

這個討厭的動詞來源於名詞 enthusiasm（熱情），不建議使用。

例如：

She was enthused about her new car.（✗）【她對她的新車很感興趣。】

She was enthusiastic about her new car.（✓）【她對她的新車充滿熱情。】

She enthused about her new car.（✗）【她對她的新車很感興趣。】

She talked enthusiastically (expressed enthusiasm) about her new car.（✓）【她熱情地談論她的新車。（表達熱情）】

38. Etc.

Literally, "and other things"; sometimes loosely used to mean "and other persons". The phrase is equivalent to and the rest, and so forth, and hence is not to be used if one of these would be insufficient — that is, if the reader would be left in doubt as to any important particulars. Least open to objection when it represents the last terms of a list already given almost in full, or immaterial words at the end of a quotation.

etc. 的字面意思是「及其他事物」；有時用得較不規範也可指「及其他人」。這個片語的意思相當於「and the rest」、「and so forth」，也就是「等等」，因此，如果列舉幾項內容中有一項不清楚，就不能使用這個片語。也就是說，在列舉的多項中，如果讀者對其中任意一項內容不清楚，都不要使用「等等」來收尾。至少要列舉到幾乎代表了整個清單內容的專案為止，或者說，只能用這個片語省略一段引言結尾處不重要的一些詞。

At the end of a list introduced by such as, for example, or any similar expression, etc. is incorrect. In formal writing, etc. is a misfit. An item important enough to call for etc. is probably important enough to be named.

such as（諸如）、for example（例如）等其他類例表達所引出的清單末尾用 etc. 是錯的。在正式寫作中，這是一個不合適的表達，因為如果某件事不重要那就不用說，但如果重要，與其用 etc. 還不如直接把事情本身說出來。

39. Fact.

Use this word only of matters capable of direct verification, not of matters of judgment. That a particular event happened on a given date and that lead melts at a certain temperature are facts. But such conclusions as that Napoleon was the greatest of modern generals or that the climate of California is delightful, however defensible they may be, are not properly called facts.

fact（事實）只能用於表達可以直接感知確認的事，而不能用於認知判斷的事。比如，發生在某天的某件事是 fact，鉛在某個特定的溫度熔化也是 fact。但是，諸如「拿破崙是現代最偉大的將領」或「加利福尼亞氣候宜人」這樣的論斷，無論聽起來多麼有說服力，都不是 facts。

40. Facility.

Why must jails, hospitals, and schools suddenly become "facilities"?

為什麼「監獄」、「醫院」和「學校」突然就成了「便利設施」?

例如:

Parents complained bitterly about the fire hazard in the wooden facility. (✗)
【家長們對木製設施的火災隱患深惡痛絕。】

Parents complained bitterly about the fire hazard in the wooden schoolhouse. (√)
【家長們對木製校舍的火災隱患深惡痛絕。】

He has been appointed warden of the new facility. (✗)【他已被任命為新設施的管理員。】

He has been appointed warden of the new prison. (√)【他被任命為新監獄的監獄長。】

4-5　常錯詞 41-50

41. Factor.

A hackneyed word; the expressions of which it is a part can usually be replaced by something more direct and idiomatic.

factor（因素、要素）也是一個被濫用的詞。如果要表達某個事物的構成要件，可以說得更直接、更符合日常表達習慣一些。

例如：

Her superior training was the great factor in her winning the match.（×）【她出色的訓練是她贏得比賽的重要因素。】

She won the match by being better trained.（√）【她透過更好的訓練贏得了比賽。】

Air power is becoming an increasingly important factor in deciding battles.（×）【空軍正在成為決定戰鬥的一個越來越重要的因素。】

Air power is playing a larger and larger part in deciding battles.（√）【空軍在決定戰鬥中發揮著越來越大的作用。】

42. Farther / Further.

The two words are commonly interchanged, but there is a distinction worth observing: farther serves best as a distance word, further as a time or quantity word. You chase a ball farther than the other fellow; you pursue a subject further.

這兩個詞通常可以互換，但是有一個區別值得注意：涉及距離的時候最好使用 farther，而時間或數量的時候最好用 further。追趕一個球時比同伴跑得遠用 farther；研究一個課題更深入時用 further。

43. Feature.

Another hackneyed word; like factor, it usually adds nothing to the sentence in which it occurs.

feature 又是一個被濫用的詞；就像 factor 一樣，它通常並沒有給句子增添任何資訊量。

例如：

A feature of the entertainment especially worthy of mention was the singing of Allison Jones. 【娛樂活動特別值得一提的特色是艾莉森‧瓊斯的演唱。】

(Better use the same number of words to tell what Allison Jones sang and how she sang it.)

（最好能用差不多長度的句子，來具體說明艾莉森・瓊斯唱的是什麼以及唱得怎麼樣。）

As a verb, in the sense of "offer as a special attraction", it is to be avoided.

而作為動詞時，feature 的意思是「以……為特色」，還是不用為好。

44. Finalize.

A pompous, ambiguous verb. (See Chapter V, Reminder 21.)

這是一個浮誇而含糊的動詞。（參見第五章的第 21 條注意事項。）

45. Fix.

Colloquial in America for arrange, prepare, mend. The usage is well established. But bear in mind that this verb is from figere: "to make firm", "to place definitely". These are the preferred meanings of the word.

美式口語中相當於 arrange（安排）、prepare（準備）、mend（維修）。這種用法已經深入人心。但不能忘記，這個動詞來源於拉丁文的 figere 一詞，原本的意思是「固定」、「確定」。與詞源相關的才是該詞最恰當的含義。

46. Flammable.

An oddity, chiefly useful in saving lives. The common word meaning "combustible" is inflammable. But some people are thrown off by the in- and think inflammable means "not combustible". For this reason, trucks carrying gasoline or explosives are now marked FLAMMABLE. Unless you are operating such a truck and hence are concerned with the safety of children and illiterates, use inflammable.

一個怪詞，主要用來提醒人們注意安全。通常表達「易燃的」含義的詞是 inflammable。但是，一些人因為看到 inflammable 之前有字首 in-，就誤以為是否定含義「不易燃的」。這就是 flammable 產生的原因。現在，運載汽油或爆炸物的卡車都標有「flammable」字樣。除非你在駕駛這樣的卡車，而且擔心小孩子或文盲的安全，否則還是要使用 inflammable。

47. Folk.

A collective noun, equivalent to people. Use the singular form only. Folks, in the sense of "parents", "family", "those present", is colloquial and too folksy for formal writing.

是一個集合名詞，相當於 people。只用單數形式。複數形式的 folks 用於口語，表達「父母」、「家人」、「那些在場的人」等等，因為太隨意而不適於正式寫作。

例如：

Her folks arrived by the afternoon train.（✗）【她的家人搭乘下午的火車到達。】

Her father and mother arrived by the afternoon train.（√）【她的父母搭乘下午的火車到達。】

48. Fortuitous.

Limited to what happens by chance. Not to be used for fortunate or lucky.

這個詞僅限於表達偶然發生的好事。不能用來代替 fortunate 或 lucky 表示幸運和運氣。

49. Get.

The colloquial have got for have should not be used in writing.

在口語中，have got 等於 have，表示「有」，但是不應該用於寫作。

例如：

He has not got any sense.（✗）【他沒有任何意義。】

He has no sense.（√）【他沒有任何意義。】

The preferable form of the participle is got, not gotten.

get 的過去分詞最好寫成 got 而不是 gotten。

例如：

They returned without having gotten any.（✗）【他們什麼也沒得到就回來了。】

They returned without having got any.（√）【他們什麼也沒得到就回來了。】

50. Gratuitous.

Means "unearned", or "unwarranted".

意思是「不勞而獲的，不應得的」或「沒有授權的，沒有道理的」。

例如：

The insult seemed gratuitous. (undeserved) 【侮辱似乎是無緣無故的。（不應有的）】

4-6 常錯詞 51-60

51. He is a man who.

A common type of redundant expression; see Rule 17.

這是一種常見的囉唆表達，具體參見規則十七的分析。

例如：

He is a man who is very ambitious. (✗) 【他是一個很有野心的人。】

He is very ambitious. (✓) 【他很有野心。】

Vermont is a state that attracts visitors because of its winter sports. 【佛蒙特州是一個因其冬季運動而吸引遊客的州。】

Vermont attracts visitors because of its winter sports. 【佛蒙特州因其冬季運動而吸引遊客。】

52. Hopefully.

This once-useful adverb meaning "with hope" has been distorted and is now widely used to mean "I hope" or "it is to be hoped". Such use is not merely wrong, it is silly. To say, "Hopefully I'll leave on the noon plane" is to talk nonsense. Do you mean you'll leave on the noon plane in a hopeful frame of mind? Or do you mean you hope you'll leave on the noon plane? Whichever you mean, you haven't said it clearly. Although the word in its new, free-floating capacity may be pleasurable and even useful to many, it offends the ear of many others, who do not like to see words dulled or eroded, particularly when the erosion leads to ambiguity, softness, or nonsense.

這個意思是「懷有希望」的曾經很有用的副詞，已經被曲解了，現在被廣泛地用於表達「我希望」或者「被期待」的含義。這種用法不僅僅是錯誤的，而且是愚蠢的。「懷有希望地，我將乘坐中午的班機離開」這句話就有些不知所云。你的意思是自己只是有期待乘中午班機離開的想法？還是自己希望乘坐中午的班機離開？無論哪種，這句話都沒有把你的意思表達清楚。儘管對於很多人來說，hopefully 的這些新的、隨意的含義是好的，甚至有用的，但還是有不少人認為它們難以接受，這些人不願意看到詞語的含義模糊或相互交錯侵蝕，尤其是這種交錯侵蝕導致歧義、欠缺表達力或者不知所云。

53. However.

Avoid starting a sentence with however when the meaning is "nevertheless". The word usually serves better when not in first position.

當用 however 表達「但是，然而」的含義時，不要把它放在句子開頭，用作插入語的方式更好。

例如：

The roads were almost impassable. However, we at last succeeded in reaching

The roads were almost impassable. At last, however-er, we succeeded in reaching camp.（✗）【道路幾乎無法通行。然而，我們終於成功地到達了營地。】　　camp.（√）【道路幾乎無法通行。然而，我們終於成功地到達了營地。】

When however comes first, it means "in whatever way" or "to whatever extent".

把 however 放到句子開頭，會帶有「無論如何」、「不管怎樣」的含義。

例如：

However you advise him, he will probably do as he thinks best.【不管你給他什麼建議，他都可能會按照他認為最好的方式去做。】

However discouraging the prospect, they never lost heart.【不管前景如何令人沮喪，他們從未灰心。】

54. Illusion.

See allusion.

illusion 的解釋參見 allusion 詞條。

55. Imply / Infer.

Not interchangeable. Something implied is something suggested or indicated, though not expressed. Something inferred is something deduced from evidence at hand.

這兩個詞不能互換使用。imply 是指沒有明說的意思；而 infer 則是根據已經掌握的證據推理出來的意思。

例如：

Farming implies early rising.【耕種意味著早起。】

Since she was a farmer, we inferred that she got up early.【由於她是農民，我們推斷她起得很早。】

56. Importantly.

Avoid by rephrasing.

這個詞不好，換成其他詞或片語來表達。

例如：

More importantly, he paid for the damages.（✗）【更重要的是，他已經支付了損失。】

What's more, he paid for the damages.（✓）【更何況，他已經支付了損失。】

With the breeze freshening, he altered course to pass inside the island. More importantly, as things turned out, he tucked in a reef.（✗）【由於風勢增強，他改變了進島

With the breeze freshening, he altered course to pass inside the island. More important, as things turned out, he tucked in a reef.（✓）【由於風勢增強，他改變了進島

的航線。更重要的是,後來他還把帆收起來了。】

的航線。此外,後來他還把帆收起來了。】

57. In regard to.

Often wrongly written in regards to. But as regards is correct, and means the same thing.

在這個片語中,regard 常被誤寫成複數形式 regards。但是,在另一個片語 as regards 中,複數形式就是正確的,意思和 in regard to 是一樣的,都表示「至於,關於」。

58. In the last analysis.

A bankrupt expression.

這個片語的含義是「總之,歸根結柢」,但實際上是一個沒有什麼價值的說法。

59. Inside of / Inside.

The of following inside is correct in the adverbial meaning "in less than". In other meanings, of is unnecessary.

表示「少於」這個含義時,inside 後面要接 of,用作狀語;而表示其他含義,如「在……裡面」,就不要接 of 了。

例如:

Inside of five minutes I'll be inside the bank.【五分鐘之內我就會到銀行裡面。】

Part 2　格式與用詞規範

60. Insightful.

The word is a suspicious overstatement for "perceptive". If it is to be used at all, it should be used for instances of remarkably penetrating vision. Usually, it crops up merely to inflate the commonplace.

在表達「有洞察力的，感覺靈敏的」這種含義時，用 insightful 是誇張到令人懷疑的。除非真的要形容極其敏銳的洞察力，才有必要用這麼誇張的詞。一般情況下，使用 insightful 就是一種吹捧。

例如：

That was an insightful remark you made.（✗）【你的評論很有洞察力。】

That was a perceptive remark you made.（√）【你的評論很透澈。】

4-7　常錯詞 61-70

61. In terms of.

A piece of padding usually best omitted.

「就……而言」這個片語是湊字數的廢話，最好刪除不用。

例如：

The job was unattractive in terms of salary.（✗）

【就薪水而言，這份工作沒有吸引力。】

The salary made the job unattractive.（✓）【薪水使這份工作沒有吸引力。】

62. Interesting.

An unconvincing word; avoid it as a means of introduction.

Instead of announcing that what you are about to tell is interesting, make it so.

在沒有說具體內容之前，就用「有趣的」這個形容詞來介紹之後的內容，是缺乏說服力的做法。與其宣稱自己要說的內容有趣，不如把內容本身說得有趣。

例如：

An interesting story is told of … (✗)【一個有趣的故事被講述……】

Tell the story without preamble.（√）（不如刪除序言，開門見山，直接說事。）

In connection with the forthcoming visit of Mr. B. to America, it is interesting to recall that he … (✗)【關於B先生即將訪問美國的事，有趣的是……】

Mr. B., who will soon visit America...（√）【B先生，即將訪問美國……】

Also to be avoided in introduction is the word funny. Nothing becomes funny by being labeled so.

同理，funny 也沒有必要出現在介紹中。你的內容不會因為你貼了一個寫著「有趣」字樣的標籤，就變得有趣。

63. Irregardless.

Should be regardless. The error results from failure to see the negative in -less and from a desire to get it in as a prefix, suggested by such words as irregular, irresponsible, and, perhaps especially, irrespective.

「無論，不管」這個詞應該刪去字首 ir 直接寫成 regardless。這種拼寫錯誤的原因，是沒有看到字尾 -less 已經有否定的意味了，再多餘新增了一個否定字首 ir-，模仿的可能是 irregular（不規範的）、irresponsible（不負責任的），尤其是 irrespective（不考慮）等詞。

64. -ize.

Do not coin verbs by adding this tempting suffix. Many good and useful verbs do end in -ize: summarize, fraternize, harmonize, fertilize. But there is a growing list of abominations: containerize, prioritize, finalize, to name three. Be suspicious of -ize; let your ear and your eye guide you. Never tack -ize onto a noun to create a verb. Usually you will discover that a useful verb already exists. Why say "utilize" when there is the simple, unpretentious word use?

不要動不動就新增字尾 -ize 來構造動詞。雖然，的確有許多好用的動詞是以 -ize 結尾的，例如 summarize（總結）、fraternize（結交）、harmonize（使和諧）、fertilize（施肥）等。但令人討厭的是這類動詞越來越多，隨便就可以舉出三個：containerize（用貨櫃裝運），prioritize（優先處理），finalize（使完成，使結束）。對於 -ize 這個字尾，還是要保留一點懷疑態度，眼界放寬一些。不要總在一個名詞後加 -ize 來構造一個動詞。通常，你會發現一個很好用的動詞已經存在了。當已經有了一個簡單、不裝腔作勢的動詞「use」時，為什麼還要用「utilize」？

65. Kind of.

Except in familiar style, not to be used as a substitute for rather or something like. Restrict it to its literal sense:

除非在非正式文體中，否則不要用 kind of（有點）這個片語替代 rather（相當）或者 something like（有點像）。要嚴格根據字面含義來使用這個片語：

例如：

Amber is a kind of fossil resin. 【琥珀是一種化石樹脂。】

I dislike that kind of publicity. 【我不喜歡這種宣傳。】

The same holds true for sort of.

sort of 這個片語也是一樣的道理。

66. Lay.

A transitive verb. Except in slang ("Let it lay"), do not misuse it for the intransitive verb lie.

這是一個及物動詞（除了在俚語「讓它躺下」中）。不要與不及物動詞 lie 混淆。

例如：

The hen lays an egg. 【母雞下了一個蛋。】

The play lays an egg. 【這齣戲很精采。】

The llama lies down. 【羊駝趴下了。】

The playwright went home and lay down. 【劇作家回家躺下了。】

注意：lay 和 lie 的詞形變化交錯重疊的地方，lie 的過去式是 lay。

lay — laid — laid — laying

lie — lay — lain — lying

67. Leave.

Not to be misused for let.

表示使動意味的 leave，不要和 let 混淆。leave 是消極不作為，而 let 是積極作為。透過以下兩組例句，來比較其差別：

例如：

Leave it stand the way it is. 【讓它保持原樣。（別去管）】

Let it stand the way it is. 【讓它保持原樣。（保持原樣）】

Leave go of that rope! 【放開那根繩子！（別去碰）】

Let go of that rope! 【放開那根繩子！（不要繼續抓著）】

68. Less.

Should not be misused for fewer. Less refers to quantity, fewer to number.

不要和 fewer 混淆。less 說的是量更少，而 fewer 說的是數目更少。

例如：

They had less workers than in the previous campaign.【支持他們的工人比例低於之前的競選。】

They had fewer workers than in the previous campaign.【支持他們的工人人數少於之前的競選。】

"His troubles are less than mine" means "His troubles are not so great as mine".【用 less 這句的意思是「他的煩惱不如我的大」。】

"His troubles are fewer than mine" means "His troubles are not so numerous as mine".【用 fewer 這句意思是「他的煩惱不如我的多」。】

69. Like.

Not to be used for the conjunction as. Like governs nouns and pronouns; before phrases and clauses the equivalent word is as.

不要當作連詞 as 來使用。同樣都是表達「像……一樣」，但是 like 是介詞，後接名詞和代詞；as 是連詞，後接片語或從句。

4-7 常錯詞 61-70

例如：

We spent the evening like in the old days.（✗）【我們像過去一樣度過了晚上。】

Chloë smells good, like a baby should.（✗）【科洛聞起來很香，就像嬰兒一樣。】

We spent the evening as in the old days.（✓）【我們像過去一樣度過了晚上。】

Chloë smells good, as a baby should.（✓）【科洛聞起來很香，就像嬰兒一樣。】

The use of like for as has its defenders; they argue that any usage that achieves currency becomes valid automatically. This, they say, is the way the language is formed. It is and it isn't. An expression sometimes merely enjoys a vogue, much as an article of apparel does. Like has long been widely misused by the illiterate; lately it has been taken up by the knowing and the well-informed, who find it catchy, or liberating, and who use it as though they were slumming. If every word or device that achieved currency were immediately authenticated, simply on the ground of popularity, the language would be as chaotic as a ball game with no foul lines. For the student, perhaps the most useful thing to know about like is that most carefully edited publications regard its use before phrases and clauses as simple error.

Part 2　格式與用詞規範

　　為把 like 用作 as 而辯護的大有人在；他們認為存在即是合理。這是語言形成、發展自然而然。這種說法也對也不對。有時候一種表達方式只是一時流行，就像某種服裝一樣。長久以來，like 被教育程度不高的人廣泛誤用；而最近，這種誤用也在有文化、有見識的人群之中流行開來，這些人覺得 like 朗朗上口，自由隨意，所以也就像文盲一樣使用這個詞。如果每一個當前在使用的詞或表達方式，僅僅因為流行就立刻獲得認可，那麼語言就會像球賽沒有犯規線一樣混亂。對於學生來說，關於 like 一詞，最需要明白的一點就是，在大多數經過認真校訂的出版品中，在片語和從句前使用 like，會被視為一種顯而易見的錯誤。

70. Line / Along these lines.

　　Line in the sense of "course of procedure, conduct, thought" is allowable but has been so overworked, particularly in the phrase along these lines, that a writer who aims at freshness or originality had better discard it entirely.

　　line 這個詞，用於表達「程序、行為、思考等的過程」這類含義，是可接受的，但是已經被使用得如此氾濫，尤其是在 along these lines 這個片語中。所以一位注重新穎和原創性的作者應該徹底拋開它。

例如：

Mr. B. also spoke along the same lines.（✗）【B 先生說的意思也是沿著這些條理。】

She is studying along the line of French literature.（✗）【她正在沿著法國文學的路線學習。】

Mr. B. also spoke to the same effect.（√）【B 先生說的也是同樣的效果。】

She is studying French literature.（√）【她正在學習法國文學。】

4-8 常錯詞 71-80

71. Literal / Literally.

Often incorrectly used in support of exaggeration or violent metaphor.

這兩個詞常常錯誤地用於修飾誇張的表達或比喻。

例如：

a literal flood of abuse（✗）【真真實實的一陣辱罵】

literally dead with fatigue（✗）【真的累死了】

a flood of abuse（√）
【一陣辱罵】

almost dead with fatigue
（√）【幾乎累死了】

72. Loan.

A noun. As a verb, prefer lend.

loan 意思是貸款，是一個名詞。表示借錢的動作，用 lend 比較好。

例如：

Lend me your ears. 【請聽我說。】

the loan of your ears 【傾聽】

73. Meaningful.

A bankrupt adjective. Choose another, or rephrase.

一個沒有價值的形容詞。換別的形容詞或片語來表達相應的含義。

例如：

His was a meaningful contribution.（✗）【他作出的是有重大意義的貢獻。】

His contribution counted heavily.（√）【他的貢獻非常重要。】

We are instituting many meaningful changes in the

We are improving the curriculum in many ways.（√）

curriculum.（×）【我們正在對課程進行許多有重大意義的改變。】　【我們正在從多個方面改進課程。】

74. Memento.

Often incorrectly written momento.

MEMENTO（紀念品）這個詞第二個字母 e 經常被錯誤地寫成 momento。

75. Most.

Not to be used for almost in formal composition.

在正式的寫作中，不可以用 most 來表達 almost（幾乎）的含義。

例如：

most everybody （×）　　　almost everybody （√）
【幾乎每個人】　　　　　　【幾乎每個人】

most all the time （×）　　　almost all the time （√）
【幾乎總是】　　　　　　　【幾乎總是】

76. Nature.

Often simply redundant, used like character.

通常就是多餘的詞，就像 character（屬性）一樣。

例如：

acts of a hostile nature （×）【敵對行為】

hostile acts （√）【敵對行為】

Nature should be avoided in such vague expressions as "a lover of nature", "poems about nature", Unless more specific statements follow, the reader cannot tell whether the poems have to do with natural scenery, rural life, the sunset, the untracked wilderness, or the habits of squirrels.

nature 應該避免用於諸如「a lover of nature」、「poems about nature」這類含義模糊的表達中。除非這些表達之後還有更具體的陳述內容，讀者是無法分辨「poems about nature」到底是關於自然風光，還是鄉村生活，日落、人跡罕至的荒野，還是松鼠的習性。

77. Nauseous / Nauseated.

The first means "sickening to contemplate"; the second means "sick at the stomach". Do not, therefore, say, "I feel nauseous", unless you are sure you have that effect on others.

同樣是跟「噁心」有關，但是 nauseous 是「令人噁心的」，而 nauseated 是自己「感到噁心的」。是完全不同的兩種含義。所以，不要把「我覺得噁心」，說成「I feel nauseous」因為這句話的意思實際是「我讓別人覺得噁心」。

78. Nice.

A shaggy, all-purpose word, to be used sparingly in formal composition.

nice 是一個含義粗略、萬能的詞，在正式的寫作中還是要盡量少用。

例如：

I had a nice time. 【我玩得很開心。】

It was nice weather. 【天氣很好。】

She was so nice to her mother. 【她對她媽媽太好了。】

The meanings are indistinct. Nice is most useful in the sense of "precise" or "delicate": "a nice distinction".

在這些例句中，nice 的含義是不清楚的。但是當表達「精確」、「細緻」這類含義的時候，nice 是最有用的。例如：a nice distinction（微妙的區別）。

79. Nor.

Often used wrongly for or after negative expressions.

經常被放在否定的表達之後使用，當作 or 來使用，這是錯誤的。在下面的例句中，第 1 句是錯誤的，修改方案可以選擇後面 3 句中的任意一種。

例如：

He cannot eat nor sleep.（✗）【他不能吃也不能睡。】

He cannot eat or sleep.（√）【他不能吃也不能睡。】

He can neither eat nor sleep.（√）【他既不能吃也不能睡。】

He cannot eat nor can he sleep.（√）【他不能吃，也不能睡。】

80. **Noun used as verb.**

Many nouns have lately been pressed into service as verbs. Not all are bad, but all are suspect.

近來，許多名詞被隨意地當作動詞來使用。不用一概加以否定，但是需要存疑。

例如：

Be prepared for kisses when you gift your girlfriend with this merry scent.（✗）【當你送你女朋友這種香水時，準備好被她親吻吧。】

Be prepared for kisses when you give your girlfriend this merry scent.（√）【當你送你女朋友這種香水時，準備好被她親吻吧。】

The candidate hosted a dinner for fifty of her workers.

The candidate gave a dinner for fifty of her workers.

(✗)【這位候選人為她的 50 名工作人員舉辦了晚宴。】

The meeting was chaired by Mr. Oglethorp.(✗)【會議由歐格索普先生主持。】

She headquarters in Newark.(✗)【她的總部設在紐華克。】

The theater troupe debuted last fall.(✗)【該劇團於去年秋天首次亮相。】

(✓)【候選人為她的 50 名工作人員提供了晚餐。】

Mr. Oglethorp was chair of the meeting.(✓)【歐格索普先生擔任會議主席。】

She has headquarters in Newark.(✓)【她在紐華克設有總部。】

The theater troupe made its debut last fall.(✓)【該劇團於去年秋天首次亮相。】

4-9　常錯詞 81-90

81. Offputting / Ongoing.

Newfound adjectives, to be avoided because they are inexact and clumsy. Ongoing is a mix of "continuing" and "active" and is usually superfluous.

這是兩個新發現的形容詞，因為它們的含義都不太明確而且詞形也較為臃腫，應該盡量避免使用。ongoing 既有「繼續」的含義，又有「進行」的含義，而且通常是多餘的。

例如：

He devoted all his spare time to the ongoing program for aid to the elderly.（✗）【他把他的業餘時間全都花在了正在進行的幫助老人的專案上。】

He devoted all his spare time to the program for aid to the elderly.（✓）【他把他的業餘時間全都花在了幫助老人的專案上。】

Offputting might mean "objectionable", "disconcerting", "distasteful". Select instead a word whose meaning is clear. As a simple test, transform the participles to verbs. It is possible to upset something. But to offput? To ongo?

offputting 也許可以表示「引起反對的」、「使人為難的」、「令人反感的」等意思。所以，還是選一個意思清晰的詞來代替它比較好。來做一個小測試，把這兩個分詞結構的詞變為原形動詞。與動詞 upset 進行比較。upset 是擾亂某事的意思，但是 offput、ongo 又是什麼意思呢？

82. One.

In the sense of "a person", not to be followed by his or her.

one 在表示某人時，其後不能接代詞他的或她的，而要用 one's。

例如：

One must watch his step.（✗）【一個人要留心他的腳步。】

One must watch one's step. (You must watch your step).（√）【一個人要留心自己的腳步。（你要留心你的腳步。）】

83. One of the most.

Avoid this feeble formula.

要避免使用「最……之一」這個缺乏表達力的套話。

例如：

One of the most exciting developments of modern science is...【現代科學最令人興奮的發展之一是……】

Switzerland is one of the most beautiful countries of Europe.【瑞士是歐洲最美麗的國家之一。】

There is nothing wrong with the grammar; the formula is simply threadbare.

在文法上，以上的例句沒有錯，只是這種模式化的表述比較老套。

84. -oriented.

A clumsy, pretentious device, much in vogue. Find a better way of indicating orientation or alignment or direction.

現在非常流行在一個詞後面用連字符號再銜接 oriented，來表達「傾向於……，以……為導向的」，但這是一種笨拙的，裝腔作勢的方式。我們可以找到更好的方式來表達這種含義。

例如：

It was a manufacturing-oriented company.（✕）【這是一家以製造為導向的公司。】

It was a company chiefly concerned with manufacturing.（✓）【這是一家主要從事製造業的公司。】

Many of the skits are situation-oriented.（✕）【許多小品是以情境為導向的。】

Many of the skits rely on situation.（✓）【許多小品取決於情境。】

85. Partially.

Not always interchangeable with partly. Best used in the sense of "to a certain degree," when speaking of a condition or state:

partially 並不是總能和 partly 互換使用。partially 最適合用於在說到某種狀態時，表達「某種程度上」的含義：

例如：

I'm partially resigned to it.【我已經部分接受了。】

Partly carries the idea of a part as distinct from the whole—usually a physical object.

而 partly 側重於表達整體中的一個「部分」的含義，通常指有形的人或物。所以以下例句中左邊的 partially 不太恰當，應該改為右邊的 partly：

例如：

The log was partially submerged.（✗）【原木被部分淹沒。】

The log was partly submerged.（✓）【原木部分被淹沒。】

She was partially in and partially out.（✗）【她部分進入，部分退出。】

She was partly in and partly out.（✓）【她一部分在裡面，一部分在外面。】

She was part in, part out.（✓）【她半參與，半觀望。】

86. Participle for verbal noun.

將現在分詞用作動名詞。

例如：

There was little prospect of the Senate accepting even this compromise. (✗)【即使這種妥協，參議院也不可能接受。】

There was little prospect of the Senate's accepting even this compromise. (✓)【即使這種妥協，參議院也不可能接受。】

In the left-hand column, accepting is a present participle; in the right-hand column, it is a verbal noun (gerund). The construction shown in the left-hand column is occasionally found, and has its defenders. Yet it is easy to see that the second sentence has to do not with a prospect of the Senate but with a prospect of accepting. Any sentence in which the use of the possessive is awkward or impossible should of course be recast.

在以上例句左邊的版本中，accepting 是一個現在分詞；在右邊的版本中是一個動名詞。左邊這種結構不常見，但是有人認為正確。但是，不難看出，左右兩邊的不同之處在於，在左邊，Senate 是中心詞，而在右邊，Senate 變成所有格形式後，成為修飾詞，其中心詞是 accepting。任何一個使用所有格後顯得彆扭，或者不能使用所有格的句子，都應該做出相應的修改。

例如：

In the event of a reconsideration of the whole matters becoming necessary, （ ✗ ）【在變得有必要重新考慮整件事的情況下，】

If it should become necessary to reconsider the whole matter, （ ✓ ）【如果有必要重新考慮整件事的話，】

There was great dissatisfaction with the decision of the arbitrators being favorable to the company. （ ✗ ）【對仲裁員作出的有利公司的判決，人們有極大的不滿。】

There was great dissatisfaction with the arbitrators' decision in favor of the company. （ ✓ ）【對仲裁員作出的有利公司的判決，人們有極大的不滿。】

87. People.

A word with many meanings. (The American Heritage Dictionary, Third Edition, gives nine.) The people is a political term, not to be confused with the public. From the people comes political support or opposition; from the public comes artistic appreciation or commercial patronage.

people 是一個多義詞。（美國傳統詞典第三版中列出了 9 種）the people（人民）是一種政治術語，不要和 the public（公眾）混淆。也就是說，政治上的支持或反對來自 the people（人民）；而藝術鑑賞或商業贊助來自 the public（公眾）。

The word people is best not used with words of number, in place of persons. If of "six people" five went away, how many people would be left? Answer: one people.

在數詞之後最好不要用 people，而用 persons。因為 people 是一個集合名詞，本身含有複數的意味。所以，假如說「6 個 people」中 5 個離開後，還剩幾個 people？答案是 1 個 people，這就不搭了。

88. Personalize.

A pretentious word, often carrying bad advice. Do not personalize your prose; simply make it good and keep it clean. See Chapter V, Reminder 1.

personalize 這個動詞表示使個人化、個性化，或者標注姓名的含義。這是一個裝腔作勢的詞，常常帶有不好的建議。不要使你的散文個性化，而要使之清晰易懂。（參見第五部分的注意事項 1）

例如：

a highly personalized affair（✗）【一個高度個性化的事件】

a highly personal affair（√）【一件非常私人的事情】

Personalize your stationery.（✗）【個性化您的信紙。】

Design a letterhead.（√）【設計信紙抬頭。】

89. Personally.

Often unnecessary.

表示「以個人角度看」，這個詞常常沒有必要出現。

Personally, I thought it was a good book.（✗）【就個人而言，我認為這是一本好書。】

I thought it a good book.（√）【我認為這是一本好書。】

90. Possess.

Often used because to the writer it sounds more impressive than have or own. Such usage is not incorrect but is to be guarded against.

一些作者頻繁使用 possess，是因為認為該詞表示擁有時，聽起來比 have 或 own 更加令人印象深刻。這種用法沒錯，但是還是要慎重。

例如：

She possessed great courage.（✗）【她有很大的勇氣。】

She had great courage (was very brave).（√）【她有很大的勇氣（非常勇敢）。】

he was the fortunate possessor of（✗）【他是幸運的擁有者】

he was lucky enough to own（√）【他有幸擁有】

4-10　常錯詞 91-100

91. Presently.

Has two meanings: "in a short while" and "currently". Because of this ambiguity it is best restricted to the first meaning: "She'll be here presently"("soon", or "in a short time").

這個詞有兩個意思，一是「過一會兒」，二是「現在」。由於會產生歧義，還是只用 presently 表示「過一會兒」這個含義好，相當於 soon 或 in a short time（要不了多久）。

例如：

He'll be here presently.（✗）【他一會兒就到。】

He'll be here soon.（√）【他一會兒就到。】

92. Prestigious.

Often an adjective of last resort. It's in the dictionary, but that doesn't mean you have to use it.

prestigious 表示「有名望的」、「受尊敬的」,要到不得不用時才用。雖然在詞典裡列出了這個詞,但並不意味著你必須要使用它。

93. Refer.

See allude. 參見 allude 詞條的解釋。

94. Regretful.

Sometimes carelessly used for regrettable:

表示(帶有主動意味的)「遺憾的」、「後悔的」。有時因為粗心大意會與表示(帶有被動意味的)「令人遺憾的」、「令人後悔的」regrettable 一詞混淆。

例如:

The mix-up was due to a regretful breakdown in communications.【混淆是由於令人遺憾的通訊中斷。】

在上述例句中,regretful 就應該改為 regrettable,意思是:混亂的原因是通訊系統令人遺憾地中斷了。(因為通訊系統不會自己感到遺憾,只能是引起遺憾。)

95. Relate.

Not to be used intransitively to suggest rapport.

不要把表示「與……有關」的 relate 一詞用作不及物動詞，來表達兩者之間關係和睦的含義。

例如：

I relate well to Janet. 【我和珍妮特關係很好。】

Janet and I see things the same way. 【珍妮特和我對事情的看法是一樣的。】

Janet and I have a lot in common. 【珍妮特和我有很多共同點。】

96. Respective / Respectively.

These words may usually be omitted with advantage.

這兩個詞通常還是省略不用更好。

例如：

Works of fiction are listed under the names of their respective authors. （✗） 【小說列在其各自作者的名字下。】

Works of fiction are listed under the names of their authors. （✓） 【小說作品列在其作者的名字下。】

The mile run and the two-mile run were won by Jones

The mile run was won by Jones, the two-mile run by

and Cummings respectively. (✗)【一英里跑和兩英里跑分別由瓊斯和卡明斯贏得。】

Cummings.(✓)【瓊斯贏了一英里跑,卡明斯贏了兩英里跑。】

97. Secondly, thirdly, etc.

Unless you are prepared to begin with firstly and defend it (which will be difficult), do not prettify numbers with -ly. Modern usage prefers second, third, and so on.

除非你準備以 firstly 開始,並有充分理由這麼做(通常這很困難),否則,還是不要在數字後面新增 -ly 字尾來排序。現代英語更傾向於直接使用序數詞第二、第三等等。

98. Shall / Will.

In formal writing, the future tense requires shall for the first person, will for the second and third. The formula to express the speaker's belief regarding a future action or state is I shall; I will expresses determination or consent.

在正式寫作中,將來時要求主語是第一人稱時助動詞用 shall,第二、第三人稱時用 will。shall 表示說話者對於未來發生的事情或呈現的狀態的信念;而 will 表示決心和認同。

例如：

A swimmer in distress cries, "I shall drown; no one will save me!" 【一位發生意外的游泳者會喊：「我要（shall）溺水了；沒人願意（will）救我！」】

A suicide puts it the other way:

如果是一位自殺者則是相反：

"I will drown; no one shall save me!" 【「我願意（will）溺水而死；誰都不要（shall）救我！」】

In relaxed speech, however, the words shall and will are seldom used precisely; our ear guides us or fails to guide us, as the case may be, and we are quite likely to drown when we want to survive and survive when we want to drown.

然而，在輕鬆隨意的談話中，這兩個詞就沒有必要那麼精確地區分了；我們聽到的理解的也許未必符合說話者的真實意圖：可能想要活下來的人因為沒人搭救而溺水了，而想要自殺的人因為被人救起而沒有遂願。

99. So.

Avoid, in writing, the use of so as an intensifier: "so good"; "so warm"; "so delightful".

在寫作中，不要把 so 用來加強語氣，如 so good（那麼好）；so warm（那麼溫暖）；so delightful（那麼快樂）等等。

100. Sort of.

See kind of.

參見 kind of 詞條的解釋。

4-11　常錯詞 101-110

101. Split infinitive.

There is precedent from the fourteenth century down for interposing an adverb between to and the infinitive it governs, but the construction should be avoided unless the writer wishes to place unusual stress on the adverb.

分裂不定式。也就是在不定式符號和其後的動詞之間插入一個副詞的結構。這種結構 14 世紀就有，但是盡量不要使用，除非是作者特別想強調這個副詞。

例如：

to diligently inquire （✗）　【認真詢問】

to inquire diligently （✓）　【認真詢問】

For another side to the split infinitive, see Chapter V, Reminder 14.

關於分裂不定式的其他情況,將在本書第 5 章的注意事項 14 中解釋。

102. State.

Not to be used as a mere substitute for say, remark. Restrict it to the sense of "express fully or clearly":

state 不能代替 say(說)和 remark(評論)。因為 state 僅僅表示「充分且清晰地表達」:

例如:

He refused to state his objections.【他拒絕陳述他的反對意見。】

103. Student body.

Nine times out of ten a needless and awkward expression, meaning no more than the simple word students.

這個片語十有八九是多餘、彆扭的表達,因為它的意思無非就是 students(學生們)。

例如：

a member of the student body（✗）【學生群體中的一員】

popular with the student body（✗）【在學生中流行】

a student（✓）【一個學生】

liked by the students（✓）【被學生們喜歡】

104. Than.

Any sentence with than (to express comparison) should be examined to make sure no essential words are missing.

任何帶有比較連詞 than 的句子，都應該仔細檢查，確保沒有遺漏必要的詞語。

例如：

I'm probably closer to my mother than my father. (Ambiguous.)【比起我父親，我可能更接近我母親。（這個句子模稜兩可。）】

I'm probably closer to my mother than to my father.【我可能更接近我的母親而不是我的父親。】

I'm probably closer to my mother than my father is.【我可能比我父親更接近我的母親。】

It looked more like a cor-morant than a heron.（✗）
【比起蒼鷺牠更像鸕鶿。】

It looked more like a cor-morant than like a heron.（✓）
【牠看起來更像是鸕鶿而不是蒼鷺。】

105. Thanking you in advance.

This sounds as if the writer meant, "It will not be worth my while to write to you again." In making your request, write "will you please", or "I shall be obliged". Then, later, if you feel moved to do so, or if the circumstances call for it, write a letter of acknowledgment.

想用這句話表示「提前感謝你」，但實際聽上去像是說：「再次寫信感謝你是不值得的（所以先說了）。」 在寫信提要求的時候，要用「will you please（您能不能）」，或者「I shall be obliged（我將不勝感激……）」提完要求之後，如果你覺得或者根據情況有必要，再寫一封感謝信。

106. That / Which.

That is the defining, or restrictive, pronoun, which the non-defining, or nonrestrictive. (See Rule 3.)

that 是限定性關係代詞，which 是非限定性關係代詞。（參見 Part 1 講解的規則三。）

4-11 常錯詞 101-110

例如：

The lawn mower that is broken is in the garage. (Tells which one.)【壞掉的割草機在車庫裡。（可能有多臺割草機，告訴對方是哪一臺。）】

The lawn mower, which is broken, is in the garage. (Adds a fact about the only mower in question.)【壞掉的割草機在車庫裡。（只有一臺割草機，只是補充說明割草機壞掉的情況。）】

The use of which for that is common in written and spoken language.

以 which 替換 that 的用法，在口語和書面語言中都很常見。

例如：

Let us now go even unto Bethlehem, and see this thing which is come to pass.【現在讓我們去伯利恆吧，看看這將要發生的事情。】

Occasionally which seems preferable to that, as in the sentence from the *Bible*. But it would be a convenience to all if these two pronouns were used with precision. Careful writers, watchful for small conveniences, go which-hunting, remove the defining whiches, and by so doing improve their work.

就像這個摘自《聖經》的句子，有時似乎用 which 要比用 that 好。但是，如果能準確區分使用這兩個代詞，對所有人都會更方便。細心的作者會注意細節，以為他們提供閱讀理解上的方便。這些作者會仔細鑑別文章中的 which，去除那些起限定性作用的 which（或改為 that），從而提升文章的品質。

107. The foreseeable future.

A cliché, and a fuzzy one. How much of the future is foreseeable? Ten minutes? Ten years? Any of it? By whom is it foreseeable? Seers? Experts? Everybody?

「可見的未來」是一種人云亦云的陳詞濫調，而且含義也不清晰。未來到底有多少可以預見的？10 分鐘，10 年，還是隨便？未來又是誰預見的？預言家，專家，還是每一個人？

108. The truth is… / The fact is…

A bad beginning for a sentence. If you feel you are possessed of the truth, or of the fact, simply state it. Do not give it advance billing.

把「事實是」用作一個句子的開頭時很糟糕的。如果你認為自己掌握了事實真相，直接陳述內容就好了。用不著事先標明。

4-11 常錯詞101-110

109. They / He or She.

Do not use they when the antecedent is a distributive expression such as each, each one, everybody, every one, many a man. Use the singular pronoun.

當先行詞是諸如 each、each one、everybody、every one、many a man 這些表示每個、個別的詞語時，之後的代詞，不要使用複數代詞 they（他／她／它們），還是使用單數代詞比較好。

例如：

Every one of us knows they are fallible.（✗）【我們每個人都知道他們難免犯錯。】

Every one of us knows he is fallible.（✓）【我們每個人都知道自己難免犯錯。】

Everyone in the community, whether they are a member of the Association or not, is invited to attend.（✗）【社區中的每個人，無論他們是不是協會的成員，都被邀請參加。】

Everyone in the community, whether he is a member of the Association or not, is invited to attend.（✓）【社區中的每個人，無論他是不是協會的成員，都被邀請參加。】

A similar fault is the use of the plural pronoun with the antecedent anybody, somebody, someone, the intention being either to avoid the awkward he or she or to avoid committing oneself to one or the other. Some bashful speakers even say, "A friend of mine told me that they…"

同樣的，當先行詞是 anybody、somebody、someone 時，之後的代詞使用複數的 they（他／她／它們），也是錯的。這種錯誤的原因是想要避免使用男他或女她的尷尬，或者不願意說明是男他還是女她。一些扭扭捏捏的人甚至會說：「我的一位朋友告訴我他們……」

The use of he as a pronoun for nouns embracing both genders is a simple, practical convention rooted in the beginnings of the English language. Currently, however, many writers find the use of the generic he or his to rename indefinite antecedents limiting or offensive. Substituting he or she in its place is the logical thing to do if it works. But it often doesn't work, if only because repetition makes it sound boring or silly.

用男他 he 來代指男女兩種性別的人稱任意一種，簡單、實用，自古就有。但現在，許多作家覺得，當先行詞的性別不明確時，只用一個 he 或 his 來指代是偏頗的，或是冒犯女性的。於是他們改用「he or she」，這在邏輯上是說得過去的。但是反覆使用「he or she」聽上去也是無聊或傻氣的。

4-11 常錯詞 101-110

Consider these strategies to avoid an awkward overuse of he or she or an unintentional emphasis on the masculine: Use the plural rather than the singular.

可以考慮用以下這些方式,來避免反覆使用「he or she」的尷尬,或是不經意間的「重男輕女」傾向。也就是,用複數而不是單數形式。

Eliminate the pronoun altogether.

第一種方式是刪除所有代詞。

例如:

The writer must address his readers' concerns. (✕) 【作者必須解決他的讀者的擔憂。】

The writer must address readers' concerns. (√) 【作者必須解決讀者的擔憂。】

Writers must address their readers' concerns. (✕) 【作者們必須解決讀者的擔憂。】

Substitute the second person for the third person.

第二種方式是把第三人稱代詞換成第二人稱代詞。

例如:

The writer must address his readers' concerns. (✕)

As a writer, you must address your readers' concerns. (√)

【作者必須解決讀者的擔　　【作為一名作者,你必
憂。】　　　　　　　　　　須解決讀者的擔憂。】

No one need fear to use he if common sense supports it. If you think she is a handy substitute for he, try it and see what happens. Alternatively, put all controversial nouns in the plural and avoid the choice of sex altogether, although you may find your prose sounding general and diffuse as a result.

如果符合常識,不必擔心用 he 有什麼不好。如果你覺得用 she 代替 he 更方便的話,換過來試試效果如何。另一種選擇是,把有爭議的名詞都用成複數,以避免性別選擇,但結果可能是你的文章顯得籠統、累贅。

110. This.

The pronoun this, referring to the complete sense of a preceding sentence or clause, can't always carry the load and so may produce an imprecise statement.

以代詞 this 來指代之前的整個句子或從句的內容,並不總是能夠指代清晰,所以可能會造成不準確的表達效果。

4-11 常錯詞 101-110

例如：

Visiting dignitaries watched yesterday as ground was broken for the new high-energy physics laboratory with a blowout safety wall. This is the first visible evidence of the university's plans for modernization and expansion.（✗）【昨天，那座裝有防爆牆的新高能物理實驗室破土動工，來訪的達官顯貴們參觀了。這是這所大學現代化發展計畫的第一個明證。】

Visiting dignitaries watched yesterday as ground was broken for the new high-energy physics laboratory with a blowout safety wall. The ceremony afforded the first visible evidence of the university's plans for modernization and expansion.（✓）【昨天，那座裝有防爆牆的新高能物理實驗室破土動工，來訪的達官顯貴們參觀了。這個儀式是這所大學現代化發展計畫的第一個明證。】

In the left-hand example above, this does not immediately make clear what the first visible evidence is.

在以上例句左邊的版本中，this 就沒有直接說明第一個明證是什麼。

4-12　常錯詞 111-123

111. Thrust.

This showy noun, suggestive of power, hinting of sex, is the darling of executives, politicos, and speech-writers. Use it sparingly. Save it for specific application.

thrust 表示推進，是一個炫耀力量的名詞，帶有「性」的暗示，是官員、政客、演說家鍾愛的。我們應該只在個別具體情況下適當使用它。

例如：

Our reorganization plan has a tremendous thrust. (✗)【我們的重組計畫有巨大的推動力。】

The piston has a fiveinch thrust. (✓)【活塞的推距為 5 英寸。】

The thrust of his letter was that he was working more hours than he'd bargained for. (✗)【他的信的推進的要旨是，他工作的時間比預期的要多。】

The point he made in his letter was that he was working more hours than he'd bargained for. (✓)【他在信中指出，他工作的時間超出了預期。】

4-12 常錯詞 111-123

112. Tortuous / Torturous.

A winding road is tortuous, a painful ordeal is torturous. Both words carry the idea of "twist", the twist having been a form of torture.

tortuous 與 torturous 這兩個詞只相差一個 r 字母，要注意詞形區分。形容一條彎曲的小路用 tortuous，而形容一場痛苦的折磨用 torturous。這兩個詞都含有「twist」扭曲的意思，因為扭曲也是一種折磨的方式。（作者的言下之意是在上述兩種語境下，都可以用詞形更簡單的 twist，也就不會造成混淆了。）

113. Transpire.

Not to be used in the sense of "happen", "come to pass". Many writers so use it (usually when groping toward imagined elegance), but their usage finds little support in the Latin "breathe across or through". It is correct, however, in the sense of "become known".

不要用 transpire 來表達「發生」或是「出現」的含義。通常，很多作家在想像中尋求高雅格調時，就會這樣使用 transpire，但是，從這個詞的詞根「spir」表示呼吸的含義來看，這種用法是沒有依據的。不過，用這個詞表示「被人知道」卻是對的。

例如：

Eventually, the grim account of his villainy transpired (literally, "eaked through or out"). 【最終，對他的惡行的真實描述還是被人們看到了（字面意思是「透漏或洩漏」）。】

114. Try.

Takes the infinitive: "try to mend it", not "try and mend it". Students of the language will argue that try and has won through and become idiom. Indeed it has, and it is relaxed and acceptable. But try to is precise, and when you are writing formal prose, try and write try to.

try 之後要接不定式。「試著去修好它」，不要說成，「嘗試並且修好它」。有學生會爭辯說，「try and do」的用法已經被認可成為習慣用語。也許是的，這種用法比較比較隨意，也可以接受。但是，try to do 還是更準確。在正式寫作中，還是寫成 try to do 更好。

115. Type.

Not a synonym for kind of. The examples below are common vulgarisms.

type 不是 kind of 的同義詞。下面例句中，左邊的版本是常見的粗鄙的用法，要改成右邊的樣式。

例如：

that type employee（✗）
【那種類型的員工】

that kind of employee
（✓）【那種員工】

I dislike that type publicity.（✗）【我不喜歡那種類型的宣傳。】

I dislike that kind of publicity.（✓）【我不喜歡那類宣傳。】

mall, home-type hotels
（✗）【小型家庭型旅館】

ssmall, homelike hotels
（✓）【小型家庭旅館】

a new type plane（✗）
【新型飛機】

a plane of a new design (new kind)（✓）【一架新設計（新種類）的飛機】

116. Unique.

Means "without like or equal". Hence, there can be no degrees of uniqueness.

這個詞的意思是「獨一無二的」。因此，不可能有不同程度的「獨特」。

例如：

It was the most unique coffee maker on the market.（✗）【這是市場上最獨特的咖啡機。】

It was a unique coffee maker on the market.（✓）【這是市場上獨一無二的咖啡機。】

The balancing act was very unique.（✗）【這個平衡動作非常獨特。】

The balancing act was unique.（√）【這個平衡動作獨一無二。】

Of all the spiders, the one that lives in a bubble under water is the most unique.（✗）【在所有蜘蛛中，生活在水下氣泡中的蜘蛛是最獨一無二的。】

Of all the spiders, the one that lives in a bubble under water is unique.（√）【在所有蜘蛛中，生活在水下氣泡中的蜘蛛是獨一無二的。】

117. Utilize.

Prefer use.

前文已經講過，表示使用、利用的動詞，utilize 不如 use 好。

例如：

I utilized the facilities.（✗）【我利用了這些設施。】

I used the toilet.（√）【我用了洗手間。】

He utilized the dishwasher.（✗）【他利用了洗碗機。】

He used the dishwasher.（√）【他用了洗碗機。】

118. Verbal.

Sometimes means "word for word" and in this sense may refer to something expressed in writing. Oral (from Latin os, "mouth") limits the meaning to what is transmitted by speech. Oral agreement is more precise than verbal agreement.

有時候,verbal 有「逐詞的」含義,也就意味著它指的是書面表達。而 oral 的詞根來自拉丁文的 os,表示嘴巴,也就意味著它指的僅限於口頭表達。所以,要表達「認同,同意」的時候,使用 oral agreement 比用 verbal agreement 更準確。

119. Very.

Use this word sparingly. Where emphasis is necessary, use words strong in themselves.

盡量少用 very 這個詞。如有必要強調,可以使用本身含義更強的詞。

120. While.

Avoid the indiscriminate use of this word for and, but, and although. Many writers use it frequently as a substitute for and or but, either from a mere desire to vary the connective or from doubt about which of the two connectives is more appropriate. In this use it is best replaced by a semicolon.

不要不加區別地以 while 替換 and、but 和 although。許多作家經常以 while 來替換 and 或 but，要麼是為了避免連詞重複，要麼是因為不確定 and 和 but 哪一個更合適。在以下這個例句中，用分號替換 while 更恰當。

例如：

The office and salesrooms are on the ground floor, while the rest of the building is used for manufacturing.（✗）【辦公室和銷售處在一樓，而大樓的其餘部分則用於生產。】

The office and salesrooms are on the ground floor; the rest of the building is used for manufacturing.（√）【辦公室和銷售處在一樓；大樓的其餘部分用於生產。】

Its use as a virtual equivalent of although is allowable in sentences where this leads to no ambiguity or absurdity.

如果以 while 代替 although，只要在句子中不導致歧義或不合理，是可以的。

例如：

While I admire his energy, I wish it were employed in a better cause.【雖然我欽佩他的精力，但我希望它能用於更好的事業。】

This is entirely correct, as shown by the paraphrase:

這個句子完全正確，意思等同於以下這句：

I admire his energy; at the same time, I wish it were employed in a better cause.【我欽佩他的精力；同時，我希望它被用於更好的事業。】

Compare:

試比較以下兩句：

While the temperature reaches 90 or 95 degrees in the daytime, the nights are often chilly.【雖然白天氣溫達到 90 或 95 度，但夜晚通常很冷。】

The paraphrase shows why the use of while is incorrect:

根據以下句子就可以解釋，替換成 while 不成立：

The temperature reaches 90 or 95 degrees in the daytime; at the same time the nights are often chilly.【白天氣溫達到 90 度或 95 度；與此同時，夜晚往往很冷。】

In general, the writer will do well to use while only with strict literalness, in the sense of "during the time that".

一般來說，作者最好還是嚴格根據字面含義，用 while 表達「就在……期間內／同時」比較好。

121. -wise.

Not to be used indiscriminately as a pseudo suffix: taxwise, pricewise, marriagewise, prosewise, saltwater taffy-wise. Chiefly useful when it means "in the manner of: clockwise". There is not a noun in the language to which -wise cannot be added if the spirit moves one to add it. The sober writer will abstain from the use of this wild additive.

不要不加區別地把 wise 用成一個假定成立的字尾，從而虛構出一大堆並不存在的單字。wise 的含義主要是「以……方式；朝……方向」，比如 clockwise 表示順時針方向。如果要給英語中的單字任意新增 wise 字尾，沒有哪個詞是不可以的，只是頭腦清醒的作者會避免這種隨意構造衍生詞。

122. Worth while.

Overworked as a term of vague approval and (with not) of disapproval. Strictly applicable only to actions:

這個片語被濫用於模糊表達同意，或者結合否定副詞表示不同意。嚴格來說，這個片語只能用於動作之前：

例如：

Is it worth while to telegraph?【值不值得拍電報？】

His books are not worth while.【他的書不值得。】

His books are not worth reading.【他的書不值得一讀。】

The adjective worthwhile (one word) is acceptable but emaciated. Use a stronger word.

把 worth while 寫到一起構成一個形容詞，是可以接受的，但是詞義比較弱，可以用詞義表達效果更明確的形容詞來替換。

例如：

a worthwhile project【有價值的專案】

a promising (useful, valuable, exciting) project【一個有前途的（有用的、有價值的、令人興奮的）專案】

123. Would.

Commonly used to express habitual or repeated action.

would 通常用於表達習慣或重複的行為。

例如：

He would get up early and prepare his own breakfast before he went to work.【他會早起，在上班前自己準備早餐。】

But when the idea of habit or repetition is expressed, in such phrases as once a year, every day, each Sunday, the past tense, without would, is usually sufficient, and, from its brevity, more emphatic.

但是如果這種重複或習慣的含義透過一個時間片語來展現時，如每年一次、每天一次、每個星期天，或者句子謂語動詞是一般過去時態，就不用 would，句子反而更簡潔有力。或者簡言之，就是概述內容用 would，具體敘述不用 would。

例如：

Once a year he would visit the old mansion.【他每年都會參觀那座老宅邸。】

Once a year he visited the old mansion.【他每年參觀一次那座老宅邸。】

In narrative writing, always indicate the transition from the general to the particular — that is, from sentences that merely state a general habit to those that express the action of a specific day or period. Failure to indicate the change will cause confusion.

在敘事寫作中，從概述到具體細節描寫的過渡總是要說清楚——也就是，從一般習慣行為的陳述句過渡到具體的某天或某段時間的行為的描述。如果不說明這種過渡就會造成意思混淆。

例如：

Townsend would get up early and prepare his own breakfast. If the day was cold, he filled the stove and had a warm fire burning before he left the house. On his way out to the garage, he noticed that there were footprints in the new-fallen snow on the porch. 【湯森總得早起自己準備早餐。如果天氣很冷,他會在離開房子之前把爐子裝滿,讓溫暖的火燃燒起來。在去車庫的路上,他注意到門廊上新落的雪上有腳印。】

The reader is lost, having received no signal that Townsend has changed from a mere man of habit to a man who has seen a particular thing on a particular day.

讀完以上這段文字,讀者會感到迷惑,因為沒有任何訊號標示出,文章已經從概述湯森的生活習慣,過渡到了具體描述他在某天看到的具體的事物。所以,要在概述完之後,具體內容開始之前,把具體事件發生的時間片語寫出來,作為過渡的標識。試比較以下版本:

Townsend would get up early and prepare his own breakfast. If the day was cold, he filled the stove and had a warm fire burning before he left the house. One morning in January, on his way out to the garage, he noticed footprints in the new-fallen snow on the porch. 【湯森總得早起自己準備早餐。如果天氣很冷,他會在離開房子之前把爐子裝滿,讓溫暖的火燃燒起來。一月分的一天早上,在去車庫的路上,他注意到門廊上新落的雪上有腳印。】

Part 2　格式與用詞規範

Part 3　寫作風格入門

Part 3　寫作風格入門

Up to this point, the book has been concerned with what is correct, or acceptable, in the use of English. In this final chapter, we approach style in its broader meaning: style in the sense of what is distinguished and distinguishing. Here we leave solid ground. Who can confidently say what ignites a certain combination of words, causing them to explode in the mind? Who knows why certain notes in music are capable of stirring the listener deeply, though the same notes slightly rearranged are impotent? These are high mysteries, and this chapter is a mystery story, thinly disguised. There is no satisfactory explanation of style, no infallible guide to good writing, no assurance that a person who thinks clearly will be able to write clearly, no key that unlocks the door, no inflexible rule by which writers may shape their course. Writers will often find themselves steering by stars that are disturbingly in motion.

至此，本書涉及的是一些正確使用英語的問題。在最後這一章裡，我們將從更廣義的角度來探討寫作風格：也就是有個性的能被辨識出來的自己的寫作風格。在這個問題上我們並沒有確切的依據。誰又能信心滿滿地說清楚到底是什麼觸發了若干詞語的組合，讓它們在思想中迸發出來？誰又知道為什麼某些音符能深深打動聽眾，而這些音符，稍加調整之後就失去了感染力？這些都非常神祕，本章要討論的就是一些神祕的有著一層薄薄的偽裝的東西。迄今為止，對於寫作的風格，並沒有令人滿意的解釋，沒有可靠的嚮導，也沒有人能保證頭腦清醒的人寫的文章就清楚，寫作的大門並無一把萬能鑰匙可以開啟，對於年輕的作家形成自己的文風也沒有不變的準則。作家們經常會感到，指引自己方向的星辰本身也在不停地運轉。

The preceding chapters contain instructions drawn from established English usage; this one contains advice drawn from a writer's experience of writing. Since the book is a rule book, these cautionary remarks, these subtly dangerous hints, are presented in the form of rules, but they are, in essence, mere gentle reminders: they state what most of us know and at times forget.

本書前幾章涉及的是一些出自既定的英語習慣用法的指導規則；這一章包含的則是從作家的寫作經驗中得到的忠告。既然這是一本講述規則的書，這些告誡、這些微妙的暗示，雖然以規則的方式來呈現，但實際上它們只不過是一些溫和的提醒：提醒的大多是我們本來知道卻經常忽視的東西。

Style is an increment in writing. When we speak of Fitzgerald's style, we don't mean his command of the relative pronoun, we mean the sound his words make on paper. All writers, by the way they use the language, reveal something of their spirits, their habits, their capacities, and their biases. This is inevitable as well as enjoyable. All writing is communication; creative writing is communication through revelation — it is the Self escaping into the open. No writer long remains incognito.

文風是在寫作過程中逐步形成的。當我們談論菲茨傑拉德的風格時，我們指的並不是他掌握了關係代詞的用法，而是他的用詞產生韻味。所有作家，透過自己的語言風格，在一定程度上顯露出自己的精神、習慣、能力與愛好。這是必然的也是有趣的。所有寫作都是為了傳遞資訊；具有創造力的寫作透過揭露來傳遞資訊 —— 把自己暴露給公眾。沒有一個作家能長期隱匿自我。

If you doubt that style is something of a mystery, try rewriting a familiar sentence and see what happens. Any much-quoted sentence will do. Suppose we take "These are the times that try men's souls". Here we have eight short, easy words, forming a simple declarative sentence. The sentence contains no flashy ingredient such as "Damn the torpedoes!" and the words, as you see, are ordinary. Yet in that arrangement, they have shown great durability; the sentence is into its third century. Now compare a few variations:

如果你不相信文風是神祕的，那就請嘗試重寫一個熟悉的句子看看會發生什麼。任何一個經常被引用的句子都行。

假定我們以 These are the times that try men's soul.（這是考驗人們心靈的時代。）為例。這是一個由八個簡短的片語成的簡單的陳述句。句中並沒有「這該死的魚雷！」這樣的時髦話，用的顯然都是一些常用詞。然而，這樣的排列卻具有很強的生命力；這個句子至今已流傳了兩百多年了。現在我們來比較它的幾種變體：

Times like these try men's souls.【這樣的時代考驗人們的心靈。】

How trying it is to live in these times!【生活在這樣的時代是多麼考驗人的心靈呀！】

These are trying times for men's souls.【這對於人們的心靈是充滿考驗的時代。】

Soulwise, these are trying times.【從心靈角度說，這是充滿考驗的時代。】

It seems unlikely that Thomas Paine could have made his sentiment stick if he had couched it in any of these forms. But why not? No fault of grammar can be detected in them, and in every case the meaning is clear. Each version is correct, and each, for some reason that we can't readily put our finger on, is marked for oblivion. We could, of course, talk about "rhythm" and "cadence", but the talk would be vague and unconvincing. We could declare soulwise to be a silly word, inappropriate to the occasion; but even that won't do — it does not answer the main question. Are we even sure soulwise is silly? If otherwise is a serviceable word, what's the matter with soulwise?

如果湯瑪斯・潘恩用上述任何一個句子來表達自己的感情，似乎都無法使之流傳。為什麼不呢？這些句子中找不出什麼文法錯誤，而且每個句子的意思都清楚。改寫後的每一個句子都是正確的，但每一個句子，也說不清為什麼，注定會被遺忘。我們當然也可以說是「韻律」和「節奏」的問題，但這也是模糊的，缺乏說服力的。或者說 soulwise 是一個不倫不類的詞，用在這裡很不恰當；但這樣的解釋也無濟於事——因為也沒能回答主要的問題。更何況，我們能確信 soulwise 是個不倫不類的詞嗎？如果 otherwise（否則）是一個有用的詞，那 soulwise 又有什麼不對呢？

Here is another sentence, this one by a later Tom. It is not a famous sentence, although its author (Thomas Wolfe) is well known. "Quick are the mouths of earth, and quick the teeth that fed upon this loveliness." The sentence would not take a prize for clarity, and rhetorically it is at the opposite pole from "These are the times." Try it in a different form, without the inversions:

還有另一個句子。這是後來的另一位名叫湯瑪斯的人寫的。這個句子並不著名,儘管出自著名作家湯瑪斯‧伍爾夫之手。Quick are the mouths of earth, and quick the teeth that fed upon this lovelines.(大地的嘴這麼快,以利齒啃噬著愛。)這個句子無法以清楚而獲得好評。從修辭來看,它和「These are the times.」有天壤之別。試用正常詞序將它改寫成下列形式:

The mouths of earth are quick, and the teeth that fed upon this loveliness are quick, too.【大地的嘴是快速的,它對愛的啃噬也是快速的。】

The author's meaning is still intact, but not his overpowering emotion. What was poetical and sensuous has become prosy and wooden; instead of the secret sounds of beauty, we are left with the simple crunch of mastication. (Whether Mr. Wolfe was guilty of overwriting is, of course, another question — one that is not pertinent here.)

改寫後,作者原意可能還在,但他原本強烈的情感沒了。詩意和激情變得呆板麻木;原本美妙神祕的聲音,取而代之以味同嚼蠟的感覺。(當然,伍爾夫是否過度描寫,那是另外一個問題,不是這裡要討論的問題。)

With some writers, style not only reveals the spirit of the man but reveals his identity, as surely as would his fingerprints. Here, following, are two brief passages from the works of two

American novelists. The subject in each case is languor In both, the words used are ordinary, and there is nothing eccentric about the construction.

對於有些作家來說，文風不僅展現個人的氣質，而且揭示個人的身分，好比指紋一樣確定。下面兩段短文摘自兩位美國小說家的作品。主題都是疲憊，用詞都很平常，句法結構也並不奇特。

He did not still feel weak, he was merely luxuriating in that supremely gutful lassitude of convalescence in which time, hurry, doing, did not exist, the accumulating seconds and minutes and hours to which in its well state the body is slave both waking and sleeping, now reversed and time now the lipserver and mendicant to the body's pleasure instead of the body thral to time's headlong course.【他仍未感到虛弱，只是沉湎於康復期的極度疲憊。在此期間，忙碌和工作都不存在。時間分秒累積，從不等人，在健康的時候，或睡或醒，人都是它的奴隸。而現在反過來了，時間搖尾乞憐，取悅於病體，而身體卻不再受時間的約束。】

Manuel drank his brandy. He felt sleepy himself. It was too hot to go out into the town. Besides there was nothing to do. He wanted to see Zurito. He would go to sleep while he waited.【曼

紐爾喝了白蘭地。他自己也覺得困了。去城裡太熱。況且，也沒什麼事要做。他想去看看蘇里托。再這麼等下去他就要睡著了。】

Anyone acquainted with Faulkner and Hemingway will have recognized them in these passages and perceived which was which. How different are their languors!

任何熟悉福克納和海明威的人都會從這兩段文字中認出這兩位作家，並能辨別出哪一段是哪一位寫的。他們表達疲憊的方式是何等的不同！

Or take two American poets, stopping at evening. One stops by woods, the other by laughing flesh.

再以兩位美國詩人為例。傍晚時分，一個停留在樹林邊，另一個和歡笑的人群在一起。

My little horse must think it queer

【我的小馬一定覺得很奇怪】

To stop without a farmhouse near

【附近沒有農舍為何停下來】

Between the woods and frozen lake

【在樹林和結冰的湖水間】

The darkest evening of the year.

【在一年中最幽暗的黑夜。】

I have perceived that to be with those I like is enough,

【我深感能和喜歡的人在一起就足夠了,】

To stop in company with the rest at evening is enough,

【能和同伴一起停下來就足夠了,】

To be surrounded by beautiful, curious, breathing, laughing flesh is enough…

【被美麗、好奇、呼吸、歡笑的肉體包圍就足夠了……】

Because of the characteristic styles, there is little question about identity here, and if the situations were reversed, with Whitman stopping by woods and Frost by laughing flesh (not one of his regularly scheduled stops), the reader would know who was who.

由於各具特色的文風,辨認作者並無疑問。而且就算把情境對調:惠特曼停在在樹林邊而佛洛斯特和歡笑的人群在一起(不是他按定期行程逗留),讀者還是可以知道誰是誰。

Young writers often suppose that style is a garnish for the meat of prose, a sauce by which a dull dish is made palatable. Style has no such separate entity; it is nondetachable, unfilterable. The beginner should approach style warily, realizing that it is an expression of self, and should turn resolutely away from all devices that are popularly believed to indicate style — all mannerisms, tricks, adornments. The approach to style is by way of plainness, simplicity, orderliness, sincerity.

年輕作者常認為文章的風格只是內容的點綴,是讓平淡菜餚變得可口的調料。但是風格並不能脫離內容而獨立存在;它與內容不可拆分,無法分離。初學者學習風格時應留心,要意識到這是一種自我的表達,所以應該堅決摒棄一切公認的表達風格的手段 —— 所有的癖好、花招、裝飾。形成風格的途徑是樸素、簡單、有序、真誠的。

Writing is, for most, laborious and slow. The mind travels faster than the pen; consequently, writing becomes a question of learning to make occasional wing shots, bringing down the bird of thought as it flashes by. A writer is a gunner, sometimes waiting in the blind for something to come in, sometimes roaming the countryside hoping to scare something up. Like other gunners, the writer must cultivate patience, working many covers to bring down one partridge. Here, following, are some suggestions and cautionary hints that may help the beginner find the way to a satisfactory style.

寫作對大多數人來說,費時費力。思想總快過筆頭:寫作就好比學如何打下偶爾飛過的鳥,當思想一閃而過時將其

Part 3　寫作風格入門

擊落。作家就是槍手，有時躲在隱蔽之處等待獵物出現，有時漫步在鄉間希望把獵物從隱蔽處驚起。就像其他槍手一樣，作家也必須培養耐性，需要築起層層蔽障才能射到一隻鵪鶉。接下來是一些建議和提示，也許有助於初學者找到風格入門的路徑。

5-1　寫作注意事項（1）

Place yourself in the background.

將自己置身幕後。

Write in a way that draws the reader's attention to the sense and substance of the writing, rather than to the mood and temper of the author. If the writing is solid and good, the mood and temper of the writer will eventually be revealed and not at the expense of the work. Therefore, the first piece of advice is this: to achieve style, begin by affecting none—that is, place yourself in the background. A careful and honest writer does not need to worry about style. As you become proficient in the use of language, your style will emerge, because you yourself will emerge, and when this happens you will find it increasingly easy to break

5-1 寫作注意事項（1）

through the barriers that separate you from other minds, other hearts—which is, of course, the purpose of writing, as well as its principal reward. Fortunately, the act of composition, or creation, disciplines the mind; writing is one way to go about thinking, and the practice and habit of writing not only drain the mind but supply it, too.

寫作要吸引讀者關注文章的意義和內容，而不是作者的情緒和心境。如果文章是內容充實且優秀的，作者的情緒和心境最終會得到展現，且代價不是損害作品本身。因此，第一條建議是：要練就好的寫作風格，從去除故意做作開始──也就是說，把你自己隱藏起來，隱身於背景幕後，無形之處。一個認真且誠實的作者不需要為寫作風格擔心。隨著你對語言運用的熟練，你的寫作風格會形成，因為你的個人風格會形成，當這一切成為現實，你會發現，打破自己與他人之間心靈和思想上的屏障變得越來越容易──而打破這種屏障，恰恰就是寫作的目的和主要回報。幸運的是，寫作或創作行為鍛鍊著思想；寫作是圍繞著思想展開的。思想與寫作的實踐和習慣之間相得益彰。

5-2　寫作注意事項 (2)

Write in a way that comes naturally.

寫作要自然流露。

Write in a way that comes easily and naturally to you, using words and phrases that come readily to hand. But do not assume that because you have acted naturally your product is without flaw.

用一種對你來說輕鬆自然的方式寫作,使用信手拈來的詞和片語。但是,不要以為自然流露的作品就沒有缺陷。

The use of language begins with imitation. The infant imitates the sounds made by its parents; the child imitates first the spoken language, then the stuff of books. The imitative life continues long after the writer is secure in the language, for it is almost impossible to avoid imitating what one admires. Never imitate consciously, but do not worry about being an imitator; take pains instead to admire what is good. Then when you write in a way that comes naturally, you will echo the halloos that bear repeating.

語言的運用始於模仿。嬰兒模仿自己父母的聲音;孩子首先模仿口語,然後才是書本內容。甚至一個作者完全掌握了一門語言之後很長一段時間,這種模仿還會繼續,因為要一個人完全不去模仿自己喜愛的東西是不可能的。不要故意模仿,但是也不用為模仿了他人而擔心;對於優秀作品,要用心盡力地學習而不只是單純豔羨。當你的寫作真的達到自然流露的狀態時,你就自信地寫出那些經得起模仿重複的內容。

5-3　寫作注意事項 (3)

Work from a suitable design.

寫作要從適當的構思開始。

Before beginning to compose something, gauge the nature and extent of the enterprise and work from a suitable design. (See Chapter II, Rule 12.) Design informs even the simplest structure, whether of brick and steel or of prose. You raise a pup tent from one sort of vision, a cathedral from another. This does not mean that you must sit with a blueprint always in front of you, merely that you had best anticipate what you are getting into. To compose a laundry list, you can work directly from the pile of soiled garments, ticking them off one by one. But to write a biography, you will need at least a rough scheme; you cannot plunge in blindly and start ticking off fact after fact about your subject, lest you miss the forest for the trees and there be no end to your labors.

第二章的規則十二也曾提及,在開始寫作前,透過一個適當的構思,以衡量文章的性質和範圍。即使最簡單的結構也需要構思,且無論這個結構如何構成。根據有些想像你會搭一個小費篷,根據另一些你能蓋一座教堂。這不意味著在你面前必須總要有一張藍圖,只是說你對自己要做的事情有最大程度的預判。如果只是列一個洗衣清單,你可以直接從一堆髒衣服著手,一件一件地挑出來。但是寫一篇人物專輯,你就至少需要一個大致的計畫;不能盲目投入,開始把有關主題的事實一件一件羅列出來,以免只見樹木不見森林,最後勞而無功。

Sometimes, of course, impulse and emotion are more compelling than design. If you are deeply troubled and are composing a letter appealing for mercy or for love, you had best not attempt to organize your emotions; the prose will have a better chance if the emotions are left in disarray — which you'll probably have to do anyway, since feelings do not usually lend themselves to rearrangement. But even the kind of writing that is essentially adventurous and impetuous will on examination be found to have a secret plan: Columbus didn't just sail, he sailed west, and the

New World took shape from this simple and, we now think, sensible design.

　　當然，有時候，衝動和情感比起構思更引人入勝。如果你深深地為情所困，正在寫一封求愛信，就最好不要試圖去組織自己的情感；聽任自己的情感雜亂無章，信可能會寫得更好——因為可能無論如何只能這樣，人的情感並不總是可以重新組織的。但是，即便這樣基本上是憑衝動貿然寫就的文章，細究起來背後都有一個祕而不宣的計畫：就像哥倫布發現新大陸，也不是盲目漂泊，而是一路向西，依據簡單，但是現在想來合理的計畫得以實現的。

5-4　寫作注意事項 (4)

Write with nouns and verbs.

寫作要多用名詞和動詞。

Write with nouns and verbs, not with adjectives and adverbs. The adjective hasn't been built that can pull a weak or inaccurate noun out of a tight place. This is not to disparage adjectives and adverbs; they are indispensable parts of speech. Occasionally they surprise us with their power, as in,

Part 3　寫作風格入門

　　用名詞和動詞寫作，而不是形容詞和副詞。當一個名詞欠缺表現力或是不準確的時候，以形容詞來修飾是於事無補的。這並不是輕視形容詞和副詞；它們也是語言不可缺少的部分，有時它們的表現力也是驚人的，

例如：

Up the airy mountain, 【上至颳風的高山，】
Down the rushy glen, 【下至長草的幽谷，】
We daren't go a-hunting, 【我們不敢去打獵，】
For fear of little men... 【因為害怕小矮人……】

The nouns mountain and glen are accurate enough, but had the mountain not become airy, the glen rushy, William Ailing-ham might never have got off the ground with his poem. In general, however, it is nouns and verbs, not their assistants, that give good writing its toughness and color.

　　高山和幽谷是足夠準確的名詞了，但是如果高山沒有搭配颳風的，幽谷沒有搭配長草的，威廉・艾靈漢姆（William Ailing-ham）也許永遠也不能順利完成這首詩。但是，總體而言，還是名詞和動詞，而不是它們的修飾語，給予好的寫作品質與色彩。

5-5　寫作注意事項 (5)

Revise and rewrite.

要檢查和重寫。

Revising is part of writing. Few writers are so expert that they can produce what they are after on the first try. Quite often you will discover, on examining the completed work, that there are serious flaws in the arrangement of the material, calling for transpositions. When this is the case, a word processor can save you time and labor as you rearrange the manuscript. You can select material on your screen and move it to a more appropriate spot, or, if you cannot find the right spot, you can move the material to the end of the manuscript until you decide whether to delete it. Some writers find that working with a printed copy of the manuscript helps them to visualize the process of change; others prefer to revise entirely on screen. Above all, do not be afraid to experiment with what you have written. Save both the original and the revised versions; you can always use the computer to restore the manuscript to its original condition, should that course seem best. Remember, it is no sign of weakness or defeat that your manuscript ends up in need of major surgery. This is a common occurrence in all writing, and among the best writers.

修改是寫作的一部分。幾乎沒有作家可以嫻熟到文章可以一稿就寫成的。通常，在文章寫完之後，一經仔細閱讀，你就會發現在材料的安排上存在著嚴重的問題，需要加以調整。在這種情況下，文書處理軟體可以在你重新調整文稿時，幫你省時省力。你可以在螢幕上選擇一段材料，移動到更恰當的位置，如果你暫時找不到恰當的位置，在決定要不要刪除之前，你也可以把材料移動到稿件的末尾處。有些作者覺得把稿件影印出來有助於他們審閱修改過程，而另一些作家喜歡全都在螢幕上修改。總之，不要怕對你已經寫出的東西嘗試修修改改。原稿和修改稿都要儲存；你總是能夠用電腦將稿件還原到最初的狀態，這似乎是最佳的修改過程。要記住，你的稿子最終需要進行重大修改，並不意味著你寫得不好或是失敗了。這種情況即使在最優秀的作家中也常有發生。

5-6　寫作注意事項（6）

Do not overwrite.

不要堆砌詞藻。

Rich, ornate prose is hard to digest, generally unwholesome, and sometimes nauseating. If the sickly-sweet word, the over-

5-6 寫作注意事項（6）

blown phrase are your natural form of expression, as is sometimes the case, you will have to compensate for it by a show of vigor, and by writing something as meritorious as the *Song of Songs*, which is Solomon's.

華麗的、修飾過度的文章是難以消化的，常常是病態的，有時甚至令人厭惡。如果華麗的詞藻、過分渲染的語言是你表達的自然流露，有時確實如此，那麼你就要寫得生機勃勃，就像為人稱頌的所羅門《雅歌》那樣。

When writing with a computer, you must guard against wordiness. The click and flow of a word processor can be seductive, and you may find yourself adding a few unnecessary words or even a whole passage just to experience the pleasure of running your fingers over the keyboard and watching your words appear on the screen. It is always a good idea to reread your writing later and ruthlessly delete the excess.

用電腦寫作時，必須警惕濫用詞藻。文書處理軟體的點選和流動可能是有誘惑力的，你也許會發現隨著自己手指在鍵盤上滑過，文字就出現在螢幕上，是一個愉快的過程，因此不經意間就增加了不必要的詞，甚至整段。重讀你寫的東西，並且果斷刪除冗餘內容總是一個好主意。

5-7　寫作注意事項 (7)

Do not overstate.

不要言過其實。

When you overstate, readers will be instantly on guard, and everything that has preceded your overstatement as well as everything that follows it will be suspect in their minds because they have lost confidence in your judgment or your poise. Overstatement is one of the common faults. A single overstatement, wherever or however it occurs, diminishes the whole, and a single carefree superlative has the power to destroy, for readers, the object of your enthusiasm.

當你言過其實的時候，讀者立刻就能覺察到，而且會認為你之前以及之後寫的所有內容都值得懷疑，因為他們對你的判斷力和冷靜失去了信心。言過其實是常見的錯誤之一。無論在什麼語境，以什麼樣的方式，只要一次言過其實就能弱化整篇文章，而在讀者，也就是你寫作熱情傾注的對象們看來，一次無所顧忌的極度誇張，對你的文章有摧毀性的力量。

5-8　寫作注意事項 (8)

Avoid the use of qualifiers.

避免使用修飾限定成分。

Rather, very, little, pretty— these are the leeches that infest the pond of prose, sucking the blood of words. The constant use of the adjective little (except to indicate size) is particularly debilitating; we should all try to do a better, we should all be watchful of this rule, for it is an important one, and we are sure to violate it now and then. We should all try to do a little better, we should all be very watchful of this rule, for it is a rather important one, and we are pretty sure to violate it now and then.

諸如 rather（相當）、very（非常）、little（很少）、pretty（很）這些修飾限定詞就像水蛭，吸食著文章中詞語的血液。除了用於描述大小，連續使用形容詞 little 尤其會弱化文章的表達力。（在以下這句話中，作者故意使用了 little、very、rather、pretty 幾個詞，對比有它們和沒有它們，句子表達效果的天壤之別，我們先去掉這幾個詞，來理解原本的含義）我們應盡力做好，注意這條規則，因為它是重要的，我們時刻都要確保不要違背它。

5-9　寫作注意事項（9）

Do not affect a breezy manner.

不要裝腔作勢。

The volume of writing is enormous, these days, and much of it has a sort of windiness about it, almost as though the author were in a state of euphoria. "Spontaneous me," sang Whitman, and, in his innocence, let loose the hordes of uninspired scribblers who would one day confuse spontaneity with genius.

如今，文章的篇幅很長，但其中空話居多，就好像作者是多麼興高采烈似的。惠特曼稱頌「率真的自我」，但他的率真卻解放了一大群缺乏靈感的三流作家，他們終有一天會誤以為率性而為就是才華。

The breezy style is often the work of an egocentric, the person who imagines that everything that comes to mind is of general interest and that uninhibited prose creates high spirits and carries the day. Open any alumni magazine, turn to the class notes, and you are quite likely to encounter old Spontaneous Me at work—an aging collegian who writes something like this:

談笑風生常常是自我中心主義者的文風，這種人想像，自己腦子裡一念閃現的東西就是所有人都會感興趣的，無拘

5-9 寫作注意事項 (9)

無束的文風能夠激勵人心,無往而不勝。打開任何一本校刊,翻到班級備忘錄,你很可能會遇到這種「率真自我」 很久之前就在發揮作用,一位年長的大學畢業生這樣寫道:

Well, guys, here I am again dishing the dirt about your disorderly classmates, after passing a weekend in the Big Apple trying to catch the Columbia hoops tilt and then a cab-ride from hell through the West Side casbah. And speaking of news, howzabout tossing a few primo items this way? 【嘿,夥計們,在這裡,我再一次八卦一下你們這群胡來的傢伙。在紐約花了一個週末,想觀看哥倫比亞隊的比賽,從西岸一路打車過來。說起新聞,先丟擲幾個大頭條怎麼樣?】

This is an extreme example, but the same wind blows, at lesser velocities, across vast expanses of journalistic prose. The author in this case has managed in two sentences to commit most of the unpardonable sins: he obviously has nothing to say, he is showing off and directing the attention of the reader to himself, he is using slang with neither provocation nor ingenuity, he adopts a patronizing air by throwing in the word primo, he is humorless (though full of fun) , dull, and empty. He has not done his work. Compare his opening remarks with the following — a plunge directly into the news:

Part 3　寫作風格入門

　　這是一個極端的案例，但這樣的文風，擴展到了大量新聞寫作中，儘管速度還沒那麼快。這個案例的作者，在這樣的兩個句子中犯了大多不可饒恕的錯誤：他顯然無話可說，只是在炫耀，想引起讀者的注意，他使用俚語，既不是出於憤怒，也非別出心裁；他丟擲「primo」一詞，顯得自命不凡，然而，儘管通篇都在開玩笑，卻還是無趣、沉悶且空洞。寫下的就是敗筆。把他的這段開場白，與以下的這段文字相比較：

　　Clyde Crawford, who stroked the varsity shell in 1958, is swinging an oar again after a lapse of forty years. Clyde resigned last spring as executive sales manager of the Indiana Flotex Company and is now a gondolier in Venice.【1958年，Clyde Crawford曾擔任大學賽艇校隊的選手。時光流逝，40年後，他再次划起船槳。去年春天，Clyde辭去了印第安納州Flotex公司銷售總監的職務。現在，他是威尼斯的一名船夫。】

　　This, although conventional, is compact, informative, and unpretentious. The writer has dug up an item of news and presented it in a straightforward manner. What the first writer tried to accomplish by cutting rhetorical capers and by breeziness, the second writer managed to achieve by good reporting, by keeping a tight rein on his material, and by staying out of the act.

這段文字，儘管循規蹈矩，但是言簡意賅，有內容而不浮誇。其作者用平易直白的方式挖掘、展示了一則新聞。第一個作者試圖透過玩弄文字以及故作的談笑風生來達到的效果，第二個作者透過緊扣素材和客觀簡明的報導就實現了。

5-10　寫作注意事項（10）

Use orthodox spelling.

要使用規範的拼寫。

In ordinary composition, use orthodox spelling. Do not write nite for night, thru for through, pleez for please, unless you plan to introduce a complete system of simplified spelling and are prepared to take the consequences.

在普通寫作中，要使用規範的詞語拼寫方式。不要把 night（夜晚）寫成 nite，through（穿過）寫成 thru，please（請）寫成 pleez，除非你想引入一整套簡化拼寫的系統，並決定承擔後果。

In the original edition of *The Elements of Style*, there was a chapter on spelling. In it, the author had this to say:

在本書的第一版中，曾有專門的一章專門介紹拼寫。在

Part 3　寫作風格入門

這一章中，曾有以下的內容：

The spelling of English words is not fixed and invariable, nor does it depend on any other authority than general agreement. At the present day there is practically unanimous agreement as to the spelling of most words.... At any given moment, however, a relatively small number of words may be spelled in more than one way. Gradually, as a rule, one of these forms comes to be generally preferred, and the less customary form comes to look obsolete and is discarded. From time-to-time new forms, mostly simplifications, are introduced by innovators, and either win their place or die of neglect. The practical objection to unaccepted and oversimplified spellings is the disfavor with which they are received by the reader. They distract his attention and exhaust his patience. He reads the form though automatically, without thought of its needless complexity; he reads the abbreviation tho and mentally supplies the missing letters, at the cost of a fraction of his attention. The writer has defeated his own purpose.

英語單字的拼寫不是固定不變的，它依據約定俗成而不是權威認證。現在，大多數的單字拼寫都已經統一⋯⋯然而，在歷史上的某些時期，有少量的單字可能同時存在多種拼寫方式。慢慢地，作為一種規律，其中一種拼寫方式開始被普遍偏愛，而那些更不為人們習慣的拼寫方式就顯得老氣

5-10 寫作注意事項（10）

而被淘汰了。時不時地，一些新的拼寫形式，大多是簡化版，會被創新者引入，可能被接受而流傳，也可能被忽視而消亡。有些不被接受的過分的簡化拼寫，實際上遭到了反對，因為閱讀它們的讀者不喜歡。這些拼寫讓讀者分散了注意力，耗盡了耐心。例如，讀到「though」的時候，讀者自動就辨識了，根本不會去想這個詞是不是有些不必要的複雜拼寫；但是當讀到「tho」的時候，卻要費心去把缺失的字母補出來，這樣做的代價就是消耗一部分的注意力。因此讓作者適得其反。

The language manages somehow to keep pace with events. A word that has taken hold in our century is thruway; it was born of necessity and is apparently here to stay. In combination with way, thru is more serviceable than through; it is a high-speed word for readers who are going sixty-five. Throughway would be too long to fit on a road sign, too slow to serve the speeding eye. It is conceivable that because of our thruways, through will eventually become thru — after many more thousands of miles of travel.

語言總是隨著重大事件發展的腳步前行。在 20 世紀，thru-way 高速公路一詞就站穩了腳跟，它因必要而產生，且明顯會繼續存在。在與 way 這個單字的組合中，thru 要比 though 簡便，對於以 65 英里每小時的速度駕駛汽車行進的讀者來說，thru-way 也是一個能夠快速讀取的詞。在高速公路指示牌上寫 throughway 太長而不適合，太慢而不能被高速行進中的眼睛捕捉。甚至可以想像，因為我們進入了有高速公路的時代，through 這個獨立副詞最終也將會寫成 thru—這只是時間問題。

5-11 寫作注意事項（11）

Do not explain too much.

不要解釋過多。

It is seldom advisable to tell all. Be sparing, for instance, in the use of adverbs after "he said", "she replied", and the like: "he said consolingly"; "she replied grumblingly." Let the conversation itself disclose the speaker's manner or condition. Dialogue heavily weighted with adverbs after the attributive verb is clattery and annoying. Inexperienced writers not only overwork their adverbs but load their attributives with explanatory verbs: "he consoled", "she congratulated". They do this, apparently, in the belief that the word said is always in need of support, or because they have been told to do it by experts in the art of bad writing.

把話說盡幾乎是不可取的。例如，在「他說」、「她回答」之類的表達後面，盡可能不要使用副詞，寫成：「他安慰地說」、「她發牢騷地回答」。讓對話內容本身去展現說話者的方式和態度。在對話中，轉述性動詞之後過多使用副詞是累贅且令人厭煩的。（轉述性動詞，也就是含義相當於「說」和「想」的一類動詞，常銜接直接引語）缺乏經驗的作者，不僅會過多使用副詞，而且還會使用解釋性動詞代替轉述性動詞，如「他安慰道」、「她祝賀道」。很明顯，他們這麼做是認為「說」這個詞總是需要一些補充修飾，或者因為他們受到了一些劣等文章的教唆。

5-12　寫作注意事項（12）

Do not construct awkward adverbs.

不要生造彆扭的副詞。

Adverbs are easy to build. Take an adjective or a participle, add -ly, and behold! you have an adverb. But you'd probably be better off without it. Do not write tangledly. The word itself is a tangle. Do not even write tiredly. Nobody says tangledly and not many people say tiredly. Words that are not used orally are seldom the ones to put on paper.

副詞很容易構造。在形容詞或分詞後新增字尾 -ly 即可。但是可能沒有副詞會更好。不要寫 tangledly，這個詞本身就是一團糟。也不要寫 tiredly。沒有人會用 tangledly 這個詞，也很少人用 tiredly。口語中不用的詞，書面語也不會用。

例如：

He climbed tiredly to bed.（✗）【他勞累地爬上床睡覺。】

He climbed wearily to bed.（✓）【他疲倦地爬上床睡覺。】

The lamp cord lay tangledly beneath her chair.（✗）【燈線在她的椅子下面糾纏在一起。】

The lamp cord lay in tangles beneath her chair.（✓）【燈線在她的椅子下面纏成一團。】

Do not dress words up by adding -ly to them, as though putting a hat on a horse.

不要透過新增字尾 -ly 來裝飾詞語，這樣做就像替馬戴帽子一樣。

例如：

overly ➡ over 【過於】

muchly ➡ much 【多】

thusly ➡ thus 【因此】

5-13 寫作注意事項（13）

Make sure the reader knows who is speaking.

要確保讀者知道是誰在說話。

Dialogue is a total loss unless you indicate who the speaker is. In long dialogue passages containing no attributives, the reader may become lost and be compelled to go back and reread in order to puzzle the thing out. Obscurity is an imposition on the reader, to say nothing of its damage to the work.

如果不指明說話的人是誰，一段對話的描寫就徹底失敗了。在沒有轉述性動詞（也就是「誰誰說」）的一段長對話中，讀者會因困惑而不得不重讀以弄明白。含糊不清是強加給讀者的負擔，更是對作品的破壞。

In dialogue, make sure that your attributives do not awkwardly interrupt a spoken sentence. Place them where the break would come naturally in speech — that is, where the speaker would pause for emphasis, or take a breath. The best test for locating an attributive is to speak the sentence aloud.

在對話中，要確保你的轉述性動詞沒有生硬地打斷對話內容。把這些轉述性動詞放在對話內容自然停頓的地方——也就是說，說話者為了強調，或喘息而暫停的地方。測試一個轉述性動詞有沒有放對地方，最好的辦法就是提高聲音朗讀該動詞之後的句子，看是否恰當，如以下的例句，左邊的版本中轉述性動詞的位置就不恰當，應該放到右邊版本中的位置。

例如：

"Now, my boy, we shall see," he said, "how well you have learned your lesson." （✗）【「現在，我的孩子，我們來看看，」他說，「你學到了多少教訓。」】

"Now, my boy," he said, "we shall see how well you have learned your lesson." （✓）【「現在，我的孩子，」他說，「我們來看看你學到了多少教訓。」】

"What's more, they would never," she added, "consent to the plan." （✗）【「更重要的是，他們永遠不會，」她補充說，「同意這個計畫。」】

"What's more," she added, "they would never consent to the plan." （✓）【「更重要的是，」她補充說，「他們永遠不會同意這個計畫。」】

5-14　寫作注意事項（14）

Avoid fancy words.

避免使用華麗的詞藻。

Avoid the elaborate, the pretentious, the coy, and the cute. Do not be tempted by a twenty-dollar word when there is a ten-center handy, ready and able. Anglo-Saxon is a livelier tongue than Latin, so use Anglo-Saxon words. In this, as in so many matters pertaining to style, one's ear must be one's guide: gut is a lustier noun than intestine, but the two words are not interchangeable, because gut is often inappropriate, being too coarse for the context. Never call a stomach a tummy without good reason.

不要使用做作、浮誇、諂媚、賣萌的詞藻。當有現成的、足以勝任的小詞，就不要用大詞。安格魯－薩克遜詞源的詞比拉丁詞根的詞要鮮活，所以就使用安格魯－薩克遜詞。這一點，文章風格的許多問題都是如此，讓你耳朵成為你的嚮導：表示腸子的詞，gut 就比 intestine 簡短易上手，但是這兩個詞不能互換，因為 gut 太粗俗，放在有些語境中不恰當。如果沒有恰當理由，也不要把表示肚子的 stomach 寫成 tummy。

Part 3　寫作風格入門

If you admire fancy words, if every sky is beauteous, every blonde curvaceous, every intelligent child prodigious, if you are tickled by discombobulate, you will have a bad time with Reminder 14.

如果你喜愛華麗的詞藻，如果你總是用 beauteous 形容天空的美麗，用 curvaceous 形容女人身材較好，用 prodigious 形容孩子的聰明，用 discombobulate 形容事情的可笑，那麼這條注意事項十四就會讓你覺得很難理解。

What is wrong, you ask, with beauteous? No one knows, for sure. There is nothing wrong, really, with any word — all are good, but some are better than others. A matter of ear, a matter of reading the books that sharpen the ear. The line between the fancy and the plain, between the atrocious and the felicitous, is sometimes alarmingly fine.

你會問，用 beauteous 有什麼不好？沒人知道確切答案。確實用什麼詞只要是對的，都沒什麼不好，但是就是有些詞比另一些更好。這是一個聽覺問題，一個讀書能讓聽覺更敏銳的問題。華麗與樸實，突兀與妥貼，其間的界限有時極為微妙。

The opening phrase of the Gettysburg address is close to the line, at least by our standards today, and Mr. Lincoln, knowingly

5-14 寫作注意事項（14）

or unknowingly, was flirting with disaster when he wrote "Four score and seven years ago." The President could have got into his sentence with plain "Eighty-seven" — a saving of two words and less of a strain on the listeners' powers of multiplication. But Lincoln's ear must have told him to go ahead with four score and seven. By doing so, he achieved cadence while skirting the edge of fanciness. Suppose he had blundered over the line and written, "In the year of our Lord seventeen hundred and seventy-six." His speech would have sustained a heavy blow. Or suppose he had settled for "Eighty-seven." In that case he would have got into his introductory sentence too quickly; the timing would have been bad.

葛底斯堡演說的開場白，就跨越了這條界限，至少按照我們今天的標準來看是這樣，林肯總統有意無意地，用「Four score and seven years ago.」這樣的表達輕描淡寫了歷經87年的災難。總統先生本可以直白地用87這個數詞，少用兩個詞，也省去聽眾計算的麻煩。但他還是覺得「Four score and seven years ago.」更順耳。這樣一來，雖有堆詞藻的嫌疑，卻達到了抑揚頓挫的效果。假如他過分越界，把這個表達換成「在耶穌紀元的1776年」。他的演說將受到重挫。又或者，假如他從簡使用了87這個數字，那麼開場白就稍顯倉促，節奏感就不好了。

The question of ear is vital. Only the writer whose ear is reliable is in a position to use bad grammar deliberately; this writer knows for sure when a colloquialism is better than formal phrasing and is able to sustain the work at a level of good taste. So cock your ear.

聽覺的問題是關鍵。只有聽覺可靠的作者才能駕馭好有意為之的不規範的文法；這樣的作者明白什麼時候使用口語比書面語更好，並且也不會因此損害到文章的格調。所以豎起耳朵！

Years ago, students were warned not to end a sentence with a preposition; time, of course, has softened that rigid decree. Not only is the preposition acceptable at the end, sometimes it is more effective in that spot than anywhere else.

幾年前，學生們被告誡到一個句子不能以介詞結尾；然而，時間已讓這條規則變得不那麼嚴格。把介詞放在句尾，不僅是可以接受的，在有些場合下甚至還有更好的表達效果。

例如：

"A claw hammer, not an ax, was the tool he murdered her with."【釘錘，而不是斧頭，是他用來謀害她的工具。】

This is preferable to "A claw hammer, not an ax, was the

tool with which he murdered her."

在這句話中，把介詞 with 放在句子末尾就比放在關係詞 which 之前更好。

Why? Because it sounds more violent, more like murder. A matter of ear. And would you write "The worst tennis player around here is I" or "The worst tennis player around here is me"?

為什麼？因為這樣聽起來更暴力，更匹配講述謀殺的語境。這是一個聽覺問題。如果要表達：「這裡網球打得最爛的是我。」這個意思時，你會用「The worst tennis player around here is I」還是「The worst tennis player around here is me」呢？也就是 be 動詞 is 之後的代詞用主格還是賓格呢？

The first is good grammar, the second is good judgment — although the me might not do in all contexts. The split infinitive is another trick of rhetoric in which the ear must be quicker than the handbook. Some infinitives seem to improve on being split, just as a stick of round stovewood does.

前一個表達用 is I 在文法上更準確，但是後一個表達用 is me 在判斷上更方便 —— 儘管不是在所有的上下文語境中都是這樣。分裂不定式是另一種修辭技巧，對這種技巧的運用，文法手冊肯定不如耳朵好用。有些不定式，to 和動詞分開使用效果似乎更好，就像柴火劈開了更好燒一樣。

Part 3　寫作風格入門

例如：

"I cannot bring myself to really like the fellow."【我真沒法讓自己喜歡這傢伙。】

The sentence is relaxed, the meaning is clear, the violation is harmless and scarcely perceptible. Put the other way, the sentence becomes stiff, needlessly formal. A matter of ear.

這個句子很隨意,但是意思卻很清楚,文法錯誤無傷大雅,且幾乎覺察不出來。要是不用分裂不定式,這個句子就會變得刻板,正規到沒有必要的程度。這還是聽覺問題。

There are times when the ear not only guides us through difficult situations but also saves us from minor or major embarrassments of prose. The ear, for example, must decide when to omit that from a sentence, when to retain it.

有時候,聽覺不僅僅能指導我們化解複雜的語境,還能幫助我們在程度不同的兩難之中做出抉擇。聽覺必須決定在一個句子中,什麼時候刪除連詞 that,什麼時候保留。

例如：

"She knew she could do it" is preferable to "She knew that she could do it" —— simpler and just as clear. But in many cases the that is needed.

在表達「她知道自己可以」這個意思時，刪除 that 就比保留要好 —— 因為更簡單明瞭。但是在許多案例中，that 是有必要存在的。

"He felt that his big nose, which was sunburned, made him look ridiculous." Omit the that and you have "He felt his big nose…".

「他發現自己的大鼻子，被太陽晒紅了之後顯得特別滑稽」，這個句子中 that 之後的從句很長，就不宜刪除連線詞 that。

5-15　寫作注意事項（15）

Do not use dialect unless your ear is good.

不要使用方言，除非你聽力過人。

Do not attempt to use dialect unless you are a devoted student of the tongue you hope to reproduce. If you use dialect, be consistent. The reader will become impatient or confused upon finding two or more versions of the same word or expression. In dialect it is necessary to spell phonetically, or at least ingeniously, to capture unusual inflections. Take, for example, the word once. It often appears in dialect writing as oncet, but oncet looks as though it should be pronounced "onset". A better spelling would be wunst. But if you write it oncet once, write it that way throughout. The best dialect writers, by and large, are economical of their talents; they use the minimum, not the maximum, of deviation from the norm, thus sparing their readers as well as convincing them.

不要試圖使用方言，除非你專注研究了自己企圖再現的一種語調。如果你使用了方言，就要保持前後一致。讀者對一個詞語或表達有兩種或更多版本的現象是沒有耐心且困惑不已的。在使用方言的時候，要根據發音來拼寫，或者至少要有創意，才能獲得不同尋常的音調轉變。以單字「once」為例。在方言寫作中，這個詞經常被寫作「oncet」，但是「oncet」看起來又好像是要寫「onset（開始）」這個詞而拼錯了。所以寫成 wunst 可能是更好的方式。但是，一旦你在文中用過一次 oncet 的拼寫，最好從頭到尾都貫穿使用這個拼寫。大體而言，最好的方言作家在方言使用上是有節制的；他們最小程度而不是最大程度地偏離標準，從而在不給讀者製造麻煩的同時得到讀者認可。

5-16　寫作注意事項（16）

Be clear.

要清晰。

Clarity is not the prize in writing, nor is it always the principal mark of a good style. There are occasions when obscurity serves a literary yearning, if not a literary purpose, and there are writers whose mien is more overcast than clear. But since writing is communication, clarity can only be a virtue. And although there is no substitute for merit in writing, clarity comes closest to being one. Even to a writer who is being intentionally obscure or wild of tongue we can say, "Be obscure clearly! Be wild of tongue in a way we can understand!" Even to writers of market letters, telling us (but not telling us) which securities are promising, we can say, "Be cagey plainly! Be elliptical in a straightforward fashion!"

清晰不是寫作的目的，也不總是好文風的主要標識。有時候朦朧會滿足文學的渴望與訴求，有些作家的語言風格就是以朦朧而不是清晰見長的。但是既然寫作是為了資訊交流，清晰就是一種優點。如果非要說寫作中有什麼不可替代的品質，最值得一提的就是清晰了。甚至對故意製造朦朧感

Part 3　寫作風格入門

或信口開河的人,我們也要說:「就算要朦朧,要胡言亂語,也要讓我聽清楚你的內容!」甚至對寫信向我們推銷證券的人,我們也要說:「就算要小心翼翼,要圓滑,也不用拐彎抹角的表達!」

Clarity, clarity, clarity. When you become hopelessly mired in a sentence, it is best to start fresh; do not try to fight your way through against the terrible odds of syntax. Usually what is wrong is that the construction has become too involved at some point; the sentence needs to be broken apart and replaced by two or more shorter sentences.

清晰!清晰!清晰!當一個句子纏繞到令你感到絕望時,最好還是刪除重寫;不要試圖想盡一切辦法勉強讓句法結構平衡。通常,問題在於句子某些部分結構過於複雜,需要拆成兩個或兩個以上的短句。

Muddiness is not merely a disturber of prose, it is also a destroyer of life, of hope: death on the highway caused by a badly worded road sign, heartbreak among lovers caused by a misplaced phrase in a well-intentioned letter, anguish of a traveler expecting to be met at a railroad station and not being met because of a slipshod telegram. Think of the tragedies that are rooted in ambiguity, and be clear! When you say something, make sure you have said it. The chances of your having said it are only fair.

含糊不清的表達不僅僅會擾亂一篇文章,還會毀滅生命和希望:高速公路上措辭含混的路牌引發嚴重的死亡事故;情書中不當的用詞讓愛人心碎;馬虎的電報給到站後滿心期待卻無人接應的旅客造成苦惱。想想這些模糊不清帶來的悲劇,然後把話說清楚!當你說起什麼事情的時候,一定要把它說清楚。反正也不會多費力氣。

5-17　寫作注意事項(17)

Do not inject opinion.

不要妄加評論。

Unless there is a good reason for its being there, do not inject opinion into a piece of writing. We all have opinions about almost everything, and the temptation to toss them in is great. To air one's views gratuitously, however, is to imply that the demand for them is brisk, which may not be the case, and which, in any event, may not be relevant to the discussion. Opinions scattered indiscriminately about leave the mark of egotism on a work. Similarly, to air one's views at an improper time may be in bad taste. If you have received a letter inviting you to speak at the dedication of a new cat hospital, and you hate cats, your reply, declining the invitation, does not necessarily have to cover the full range of your emotions. You must make it clear that you will not attend, but you do not have to let fly at cats. The writer of the letter asked a civil question; attack cats, then, only if you can do so with good humor, good taste, and in such a way that your answer will be courteous as well as responsive. Since you are out of sympathy with cats, you may quite properly give this as a reason for not appearing at the dedicatory ceremonies of a cat hospital. But bear in mind that your opinion of cats was not sought, only your services as a speaker. Try to keep things straight.

除非有充分的理由，否則不要在文章中穿插觀點。我們所有人幾乎對所有事物都有自己的觀點，也有極大的衝動想丟擲這些觀點。然而，動不動就大肆宣揚個人觀點，意味著這種需求是迫切的，但也許這些表達觀點的需求與論文字身毫無關係。不分場合地宣揚個人觀點是為了在一個作品中留下個人印記。同樣，不合時宜地宣揚個人觀點也許是俗氣的。就好比，你收到一封信邀請你在一家貓咪醫院新落成典禮上致辭，然而你討厭貓，那麼你回絕邀請就好了，沒有必要把你的所有情緒全都宣洩一通。你必須明確說明自己不會參加，但是沒有必要對貓進行謾罵。寫邀請函的人禮貌地向你提出要求，你禮貌地回覆他就可以了；攻擊貓，就算用的是幽默、高格調的方式，就是不相干的了。要是因為出於對貓的同情，你也許還可以將之作為不去參加的恰當理由提出。但是要記住，對方的主旨只是邀請你去演講，要針對這一點切中要害，不要扯到貓的話題上去。

5-18 寫作注意事項（18）

Use figures of speech sparingly.

要適量使用比喻。

The simile is a common device and a useful one, but similes coming in rapid fire, one right on top of another, are more distracting than illuminating. Readers need time to catch their breath; they can't be expected to compare everything with something else, and no relief in sight. When you use metaphor, do not mix it up. That is, don't start by calling something a swordfish and end by calling it an hourglass.

明喻雖說是一種常見而有用的表達手段，但是連珠炮式地連續使用明喻，就成了干擾而不是讓人更易於理解了。讀者需要有喘息的時間；不能指望他們把所有事物都與另一些事物關聯比較，而且眼睛沒有片刻休息。當你使用暗喻的時候，不要混亂。也就是說，不要一開始把某個東西用「劍魚」來指代，之後又換成了「沙漏」。

5-19　寫作注意事項（19）

Do not take shortcuts at the cost of clarity.

不要簡短到影響清晰。

Do not use initials for the names of organizations or movements unless you are certain the initials will be readiiy understood. Write things out. Not everyone knows that MADD means Mothers Against Drunk Driving, and even if everyone did, there are babies being born every minute who will someday encounter the name for the first time. They deserve to see the words, not simply the initials. A good rule is to start your article by writing out names in full, and then, later, when your readers have got their bearings, to shorten them.

不要使用首字母縮略詞來表示組織或運動的名稱，除非你確定這個首字母縮詞讀者會一目了然。還是寫完整所有單字比較好。不是每個人都知道 MADD 意思是反酒駕母親聯盟，而且就算現在的每個人都知道，也還有每分鐘都在出生嬰兒，將來某天可能會第一次看到這個詞。應該讓他們看到每一個完整的單字，而不是一組縮略的字母。好的做法是在文章開頭寫出全名，當讀者熟悉了以後再進行首字母縮略。

Many shortcuts are self-defeating; they waste the reader's time instead of conserving it. There are all sorts of rhetorical stratagems and devices that attract writers who hope to be pithy, but most of them are simply bothersome. The longest way round is usually the shortest way home, and the one truly reliable shortcut in writing is to choose words that are strong and surefooted to carry readers on their way.

許多首字母縮略詞都適得其反；它們浪費了讀者的時間而不是節約。各式各樣的修辭策略和手段，對於希望文章精練的作者都是有吸引力的，但是它們中的大多數都只令人困擾。最長的路往往就是回家的捷徑，寫作中真正的簡潔是選擇那些表達力強、含義明確的詞，呈現給讀者。

5-20　寫作注意事項 (20)

Avoid foreign languages.

避免使用外語。

The writer will occasionally find it convenient or necessary to borrow from other languages. Some writers, however, from sheer exuberance or a desire to show off, sprinkle their work liberally with foreign expressions, with no regard for the reader's comfort. It is a bad habit. Write in English.

作者有時候會覺得借用外語表達是方便的。但是有些作者，不顧讀者的感受，純粹為了複雜化和炫耀，故意地在表達中夾雜外語。這是一個壞習慣。還是要用英語寫作比較好。

5-21　寫作注意事項（21）

Prefer the standard to the offbeat.

寧可循規蹈矩也不標新立異。

Young writers will be drawn at every turn toward eccentricities in language. They will hear the beat of new vocabularies, the exciting rhythms of special segments of their society, each speaking a language of its own. All of us come under the spell of these unsettling drums; the problem for beginners is to listen to them, learn the words, feel the vibrations, and not be carried away.

年輕作者動輒就使用離經叛道的語言。他們能捕捉到新詞，跟隨自己圈子裡特別的語言片段令人興奮的節奏，而每個圈子都在說著自己的語言。我們都會聽到這樣一陣陣令人不安的聲音；對初學者來說，問題是要聽這些聲音，學習這些詞彙，感受到語言的波動，但是不要隨波逐流。

Youths invariably speak to other youths in a tongue of their own devising: they renovate the language with a wild vigor, as they would a basement apartment. By the time this paragraph sees print, psyched, nerd, ripoff, dude, geek, and funky will be the words of yesteryear, and we will be fielding more recent ones that have come bouncing into our speech — some of them into our dictionary as well. A new word is always up for survival. Many do survive. Others grow stale and disappear. Most are, at least in their infancy, more appropriate to conversation than to composition.

年輕人互相交談時總喜歡用他們自己發明的語言：他們以狂野的熱情革新語言，就像改造自己公寓的地下室一樣。到本書出版的時刻為止，psyched（激動的）、nerd（呆子）、ripoff（搶奪）、dude（小子）、geek（蠢貨）和funky（時髦的）等等這些新發明的詞都即將成為明日黃花，更新的詞彙一直躍入我們的眼簾，進入我們的語言 —— 它們中的一些甚至會被收入詞典。新詞總想沿用下去，許多確實得以沿用了，但也有一些過氣、消失。大多數的新詞，至少在它們產生的初期，更適合用在口語而不是寫作中。

Part 3　寫作風格入門

Today, the language of advertising enjoys an enormous circulation. With its deliberate infractions of grammatical rules and its crossbreeding of the parts of speech, it profoundly influences the tongues and pens of children and adults.

如今，廣告用語十分流行。廣告語故意打破文法規則，混搭語言片段，深刻地影響著孩子和成年人的口語以及書面語。

例如：

Your new kitchen range is so revolutionary it obsoletes all other ranges. 【你的廚房新的陳列方式如此具有革命性，它淘汰了其他所有的陳列方式。】

Your counter top is beautiful because it is accessorized with gold-plated faucets. 【你的檯面很美觀，因為它配備了鍍金水龍頭。】

Your cigarette tastes good like a cigarette should. 【你的香菸抽起來才像是香菸的本來味道。】

And, like the man says, you will want to try one. You will also, in all probability, want to try writing that way, using that language. You do so at your peril, for it is the language of mutilation.

5-21 寫作注意事項（21）

　　就像廣告詞中所說的，你會想試一試。你會想，只要有可能，也要嘗試用這種表達方式來寫作。不過你這麼做也有風險，因為這是一種殘破的語言。

　　Advertisers are quite understandably interested in what they call "attention getting". The man photographed must have lost an eye or grown a pink beard, or he must have three arms or be sitting wrong-end-to on a horse. This technique is proper in its place, which is the world of selling, but the young writer had best not adopt the device of mutilation in ordinary composition, whose purpose is to engage, not paralyze, the readers' senses. Buy the gold-plated faucets if you will, but do not accessorize your prose. To use the language well, do not begin by hacking it to bits; accept the whole body of it, cherish its classic form, its variety, and its richness.

　　廣告人對他們所謂的「注意力獲取」非常感興趣，這是可以理解的。照片上的人必須只有一隻眼睛，或者長了粉紅色的鬍子，三條手臂，倒騎著馬。這些吸引注意力的技巧在商業廣告中是恰當的，但是年輕的作者在一般的寫作中，最好不要使用這樣支離破碎的表達手段，因為他們寫作的目的，是要符合而不是瓦解讀者的理智。買鍍金水龍頭這樣的事情你儘可以隨心所欲，但是文章還是不要穿鑿附會為好。為了把語言用好，開始就不要打碎它；把語言作為一個整體去接受，珍重經典形式、變化和豐富性。

Another segment of society that has constructed a language of its own is business. People in business say that toner cartridges are in short supply, that they have updated the next shipment of these cartridges, and that they will finalize their recommendations at the next meeting of the board. They are speaking a language familiar and dear to them. Its portentous nouns and verbs invest ordinary events with high adventure; executives walk among toner cartridges, caparisoned like knights. We should tolerate them — every person of spirit wants to ride a white horse. The only question is whether business vocabulary is helpful to ordinary prose. Usually, the same ideas can be expressed less formidably, if one makes the effort. A good many of the special words of business seem designed more to express the user's dreams than to express a precise meaning. Not all such words, of course, can be dismissed summarily; indeed, no word in the language can be dismissed offhand by anyone who has a healthy curiosity. Update isn't a bad word; in the right setting it is useful. In the wrong setting, though, it is destructive, and the trouble with adopting coinages too quickly is that they will bedevil one by insinuating themselves where they do not belong. This may sound like rhetorical snobbery, or plain stuffiness; but you will discover, in the course of your work, that the setting of a word is just as restrictive as the setting of a jewel. The general rule here is to prefer the standard. Finalize, for instance, is not standard; it is special, and it is a peculiarly fuzzy and silly word. Does it mean "terminate", or does it mean "put into final form"? One can't be sure, really, what it means, and one gets the impression that the person using it doesn't know, either, and doesn't want to know.

另一個已經形成自己獨特語言方式的是商人圈子。商人們在說到列印機墨盒缺貨時用片語 in short supply，說已經發出下一批墨盒的時候用動詞 update，說到在下一次董事會上要把推薦的事情最終確定下來用動詞 finalize。他們在使用的是一種在自己的圈子裡熟悉而親切的語言。但其中裝腔作勢的名詞和動詞卻使平常的事情聽上去像是有很大風險，行走在列印機墨盒間的商人們，彷彿穿戴整齊的騎士。我們應該寬容他們——每一個鬥志昂揚的人都幻想過自己騎著白馬的情景。唯一的問題是，商業用語是否也適用於一般寫作呢？通常，如果花點心思，同樣的意思也可以表達得不那麼令人望而生畏。大量的商業術語都似乎是設計出來描述商人自己的夢想，而不是用來把意思說清楚的。當然，並不是說這些詞語要通通排除；的確，語言中沒有哪個詞會被有著正常好奇心的人，不假思索地排除。update 不是一個壞詞，在恰當的語境中,它是有用的。但在不恰當的語境中,它就是一個災難。草率地採用生造詞的麻煩就在於,它們突兀地出現在不該出現的地方,會讓讀者產生困惑。這聽上去也許像一個在修辭上刻板的勢利鬼說的話;但是你會發現,在你寫作的過程中,詞語的安排就像珠寶的排列一樣嚴格。普遍法則還是偏向標準化。例如 finalize 這個詞就是不標準的,它是很特別,但卻是一個模糊、傻氣的怪詞。它的意思是「終結」,還是「最終成形」呢?人們是不確定的,人們覺得使用這個詞的人,自己也不知道,甚至不想知道。

The special vocabularies of the law, of the military, of the government are familiar to most of us. Even the world of criticism has a modest pouch of private words (luminous, taut), whose only virtue is that they are exceptionally nimble and can escape from the garden of meaning over the wall. Of these critical words, Wolcott Gibbs once wrote, "… they are detached from the language and inflated like little balloons." The young writer should learn to spot them — words that at first glance seem freighted with delicious meaning but that soon burst in air, leaving nothing but a memory of bright sound.

法律、軍事、政治專業詞彙為我們大多數人所熟知。甚至評論界也有少量的詞 [如 luminous(清楚的)、taut(整潔的)],其唯一優點就是格外靈活,可以有言外之意。對於

5-21 寫作注意事項（21）

這些批評用詞，沃爾科特・吉布斯（Wolcott Gibbs）曾寫道，「……它們脫離常規語言，像一個個充滿氣的小氣球。」年輕的作家們應該學會辨識這些詞 —— 這些詞乍看之下含義豐富，但不久就如氣球在空氣中爆炸，除了一聲響什麼也沒留下。

The language is perpetually in flux: it is a living stream, shifting, changing, receiving new strength from a thousand tributaries, losing old forms in the backwaters of time. To suggest that a young writer not swim in the main stream of this turbulence would be foolish indeed, and such is not the intent of these cautionary remarks. The intent is to suggest that in choosing between the formal and the informal, the regular and the offbeat, the general and the special, the orthodox and the heretical, the beginner err on the side of conservatism, on the side of established usage. No idiom is taboo, no accent forbidden; there is simply a better chance of doing well if the writer holds a steady course, enters the stream of English quietly, and does not thrash about.

語言永遠在變化：它是一條歡騰的溪流，轉換、改變、吸收著成千上萬的支流彙集的能量，在時間的漩渦中盪滌著陳舊。讓年輕人不要在它湍急的洪流中游弋是愚蠢的，這也不是以上這些告誡的目的所在。這些告誡的目的，是讓年輕人在正式與非正式、規範與不規範、普遍與個別、正統與山

Part 3　寫作風格入門

寨之間做好權衡，初學者的錯誤在於偏離傳統、既成的語言正規化。沒有什麼習語是禁區，也沒有什麼發音是被禁止的；只不過，如果一個作家穩紮穩打，不吵不鬧，讓自己匯入語言的大流之中，寫出好東西的機率會更大些。

"But," you may ask, "what if it comes natural to me to experiment rather than conform? What if I am a pioneer, or even a genius?" Answer: then be one. But do not forget that what may seem like pioneering may be merely evasion, or laziness — the disinclination to submit to discipline. Writing good standard English is no cinch, and before you have managed it you will have encountered enough rough country to satisfy even the most adventurous spirit.

「但是，」你也許會問，「要是我天性喜歡創新而不是守舊又該怎麼辦呢？要是我是一個先鋒，甚至是一個天才呢？」回答是：那就隨性而為。但是不要忘記，看上去顯得先鋒的語言也許只不過是逃避或懶惰罷了——不願意接受規則。寫好標準的英文也不是容易的事，在你能夠駕馭它之前，你將遇見的艱難險阻也足以滿足最大的冒險精神了。

Style takes its final shape more from attitudes of mind than from principles of composition, for, as an elderly practitioner once remarked, "Writing is an act of faith, not a trick of grammar." This moral observation would have no place in a rule book were it not that style is the writer, and therefore what you are, rather than what you know, will at last determine your style. If you write, you must believe — in the truth and worth of the scrawl, in the ability of the reader to receive and decode the message. No one can write decently who is distrustful of the reader's intelligence, or whose attitude is patronizing.

寫作風格最終形成於心態而不是寫作原則。正如一位前輩曾經評論道,「寫作是踐行信仰,而非玩弄文法。」這樣的良心評論不會出現在文法書裡,「文如其人」這樣的論斷也不會。所以說,「你是誰」而不是「你知道什麼」,將決定你的寫作風格。如果你寫作,你就要相信 —— 相信寫作的真誠和價值,相信讀者解讀資訊的能力。對讀者智慧缺乏信心的人、態度高高在上的人是不能寫好文章的。

Many references have been made in this book to "the reader", who has been much in the news. It is now necessary to warn you that your concern for the reader must be pure: you must sympathize with the reader's plight (most readers are in trouble about half the time) but never seek to know the reader's wants. Your whole duty as a writer is to please and satisfy yourself, and the true writer always plays to an audience of one. Start sniffing the air, or glancing at the Trend Machine, and you are as good as dead, although you may make a nice living.

本書多次提到「讀者」。有必要提醒作者,你對讀者的關心必須是純粹的:你必須同情讀者的困境(大多讀者多半時間有困境),但是永遠不要探究讀者想要什麼。作者的全部職責是愉悅並滿足自己,所以真正的作家總是只滿足一類觀眾的胃口。如果一開始,一個作家就嗅出了社會風氣,看到了社會潮流,他將變得了無生氣,儘管他可能過上舒適的生活。

Full of belief, sustained and elevated by the power of purpose, armed with the rules of grammar, you are ready for exposure. At this point, you may well pattern yourself on the fully exposed cow of Robert Louis Stevenson's rhyme. This friendly and commendable animal, you may recall, was "blown by all the winds that pass /And wet with all the showers". And so must you as a young writer be. In our modern idiom, we would say that you must get wet all over. Mr. Stevenson, working in a plainer style, said it with felicity, and suddenly one cow, out of so many, received the gift of immortality. Like the steadfast writer, she is at home in the wind and the rain; and, thanks to one moment of felicity, she will live on and on and on.

5-21 寫作注意事項（21）

　　滿懷信念，仰仗目標的力量，以文法規則作為武器，你就可以握筆出征了。這個時刻，你大可把自己類比為 Robert Louis Stevenson 詩歌中的乳牛。你也許會回想起來，這種友善、值得稱讚的動物「經歷了風吹，經歷了雨打」。就像作為年輕作家的你，必須經歷現代語言的洗禮，才能寫出不朽的著作。最堅定的作家，人在屋簷下，卻經歷著風雨，她的幸福，就是在作品中永遠延續著生命。

Part 3　寫作風格入門

參考書目

[1] WADDELL L A. *The Aryan Origin of the Alphabet—Disclosing the Sumero-Phoenician Parentage of our Letters Ancient and Modern*[M]. Literary Licensing, LLC. 2013.

[2] SACKS D. *Letter Perfect: The Marvelous History of Our Alphabet From A to Z*[M]. Broadway, 2004.

[3] LINDSTROMBERG S. *English Prepositions Explained*[M]. John Benjamins Publishing Company, 2010.

[4] PARTRIDGE E, Origins. *A Short Etymological Dictionary of Modern English*[M]. Routledge, 2008.

[5] DEVLIN J. *How to Speak and Write Correctly*[M]. Arc Manor, 2007.

[6] SWINTON W. *New Word Analysis or School Etymology of English Derivative Words*[M]. BiblioLife, 2009.

[7] DOUSE, Thomas Le Marchant. *Grimm's Law*[M].BiblioLife, 2008.

[8] LEWIS N. *Word Power Made Easy*[M].Anchor, 2014.

國家圖書館出版品預行編目資料

英語章法（The Elements of Style）——從句子到文章：從細節到整體，幫助你寫出精準、簡潔且兼具說服力的文章 / [美]威廉・史壯克（William Strunk Jr.）原著. 楊篳璐 譯著 -- 第一版. -- 臺北市：財經錢線文化事業有限公司, 2025.09
面；　公分
POD 版
譯自：The elements of style
ISBN 978-626-408-379-9(平裝)
1.CST: 英語 2.CST: 寫作法
805.17　　　　　　　114013021

英語章法（The Elements of Style）——從句子到文章：從細節到整體，幫助你寫出精準、簡潔且兼具說服力的文章

原　　著：[美]威廉・史壯克（William Strunk Jr.）
譯　　著：楊篳璐
發 行 人：黃振庭
出 版 者：財經錢線文化事業有限公司
發 行 者：崧燁文化事業有限公司
E - m a i l：sonbookservice@gmail.com
粉 絲 頁：https://www.facebook.com/sonbookss/
網　　址：https://sonbook.net/
地　　址：台北市中正區重慶南路一段 61 號 8 樓
8F., No.61, Sec. 1, Chongqing S. Rd., Zhongzheng Dist., Taipei City 100, Taiwan
電　　話：(02) 2370-3310　傳　　真：(02) 2388-1990
律師顧問：廣華律師事務所 張珮琦律師

-版權聲明-
本書版權為中國經濟出版社所有授權財經錢線文化事業有限公司獨家發行繁體字版電子書及紙本書。若有其他相關權利及授權需求請與本公司聯繫。
未經書面許可，不得複製、發行。

定　　價：375 元
發行日期：2025 年 09 月第一版
◎本書以 POD 印製